They were so silent, it seemed to Alisa that nobody even breathed as they approached the door to the visitors' lounge. Then they were there, and they saw her.

She sat in a familiar pose with her legs drawn up, her feet half tucked under her in the chair, reading a magazine. In the light from the reading lamp, her silky, dark brown hair framed her face in delicate waves, and she wore makeup, as she'd always done when she was well. Slender and lovely, she was wearing the pretty floral print dress that Alisa had packed along with nightgowns and toilet articles on that night when it had seemed as if she would never again take an interest in her appearance.

Alisa felt tears stinging her eyes. She had never before realized with such joy that her mother was so very beautiful.

"Mama!" Marty and Darlene cried at once, rushing to her and throwing their arms around her. Their mother dropped the magazine and straightened in the chair, drawing them to her fiercely, her marvelous eyes brimming. . . .

THE HAPPINESS SEED

Nadine Roberts

FAWCETT JUNIPER • NEW YORK

RLI: $\dfrac{\text{VL 6 \& up}}{\text{IL 7 \& up}}$

A Fawcett Juniper Book
Published by Ballantine Books
Copyright © 1992 by Nadine Roberts

All rights reserved under International and Pan-American Copyright Conventions. Published in the United States by Ballantine Books, a division of Random House, Inc., New York, and simultaneously in Canada by Random House of Canada Limited, Toronto.

Library of Congress Catalog Card Number: 91-93160

ISBN 0-449-70402-5

Manufactured in the United States of America

First Edition: April 1992

Chapter One

"YOUR APPEARANCE UPON this earth, in this life—was it a thoughtless, unimportant accident, or was your birth a precisely ordained part of the master plan of the universe?" Mr. Reed had asked the question during seventh-hour English III, and Alisa Wilson couldn't stop thinking about it.

Master plan? Whom had he thought he was kidding? she wondered. With the whole world in such a mess, not to mention her own life in South Rutland, how could she possibly believe there'd ever been a master plan for *anything*?

But that was Mr. Reed for you, she admitted with a perplexed frown. Always curious and interested and always digging into things, Mr. Reed was at least never boring and probably never bored. He could certainly come up with some peculiar ideas, though. A person would think that by the time someone had lived to the age of thirty-five or so, he would know better than to be so idealistic. Reality was easier, even if it wasn't so pleasant as imagining that somebody up there actually cared. At least there weren't so many disappointments if one was careful not to expect flowers to be blooming all the time.

Few flowers were blooming in Rutland, although it was springtime. In the first place, nobody in the whole south side of town had ever made more than a sporadic halfhearted effort to plant any. That left only the accidental clump of scrawny jonquils or an occasional yellow forsythia bush that was hardy enough to survive the trampling of children's play or the clutter of discarded tires and broken-down and rusting automobiles and washing machines. In the second place, a late freeze had turned the surviving few blossoms a sickly brown.

A tin can whose label proclaimed that it had once contained pork and beans lay on the broken sidewalk. Alisa nudged it off the walk and into the grass and shifted her armload of schoolbooks to a more comfortable position as she walked on.

Glancing surreptitiously ahead and to her left, she saw Mrs. Carter sitting on a straight kitchen chair on her cluttered front porch. Why hadn't she thought to take the longer way and avoid Mrs. Carter? She would be sure to have heard what had happened by now and would be wanting all the details. Her nosiness would, Alisa expected, be poorly concealed behind her protest of honest *concern* for the Wilson family. Darn Mr. Reed, anyway! His provocative foolishness had occupied her thoughts and made her forget about Mrs. Carter, perched like a vulture on that crummy porch and watching for whatever bits of raw flesh might still be exposed.

But there were Mrs. Carters everywhere. Might

as well get it over with, Alisa conceded, straightening her shoulders. They weren't all like this one, a lazy fat woman living in squalor on her dead husband's social security and finding the only sauce for her life in other people's heartaches. Still, everybody wanted to *know*, though hardly anyone ever actually asked. No doubt they meant to be kind by pretending nothing was wrong. The trouble was that she could always tell if they'd already heard something, so when they didn't ask about her mother, she couldn't bring it up herself—could she?—making *them* feel uncomfortable. Even when they had themselves convinced that they were being kind by not asking straight out, Alisa could always see it in their eyes.

Mrs. Carter wasn't too kind.

"Have a good day at school?" she asked before Alisa had even reached the corner of her yard.

"It was fine, Mrs. Carter."

"It wasn't so fine for me," Mrs. Carter whined eagerly. "Nothin's easy when you get to be my age. My bones ache, and that's a fact. Can't hardly get around to get my cleanin' done. The world is full of troubles, seems like. Heard your mama took sick again. Sheriff come for her?"

"Yes, last night," Alisa said, resigned, "but we're hoping it's not so bad this time. Maybe she won't have to stay so long."

" 'Sa shame," Mrs. Carter mumbled. "Personally, I think it's the medicine that makes her go off like that. All them drugs can't be good for a body. But then, I ain't no doctor, neither. I just hope it don't last. I worry so much about you children!"

3

"We're fine, Mrs. Carter," Alisa said through clenched teeth. "We aren't exactly alone, you know."

"Well, no, I reckon you ain't, but . . ."

"I have to get home," Alisa said abruptly. "Marty and Darlene will be there any time." And she walked away, leaving Mrs. Carter to think what she pleased.

It was true enough: She did need to hurry, for her brother and sister would be coming home from elementary school, and she wanted to make the evening as easy for them as she could. Young as they were, with Marty in kindergarten and Darlene in second grade, they had recognized the signs of their mother's approaching collapse just as she and their father had; they had seen it before. And even if there was a horribly guilty sense of relief that it finally *had* happened, they would miss their mother's presence in the house.

But probably Marty and Darlene didn't experience that relief and the almost intolerably weighty guilt that came with it, Alisa considered. She hoped that they only missed their mother, and Meredith Wilson was a terrific mother, the best in the world when she was well. Only this was the third time she'd been sick in less than two years.

Deliberately, Alisa forced her thoughts away from the heavy question of her mother's illness, for which there seemed to be no answers. She would fix a nice supper and see that the kids did their homework. Maybe it was a bit of a strain on her patience to watch Marty laboring over the endless repetition of writing his numbers, but seeing his eyes light up with the pleasure of his accomplishment made it worth the time. Darlene would almost certainly bring home a new book to read, but her father would be a willing audience for that, holding Darlene in his lap, holding back his impatient urge to pronounce the hard words for her.

Her steps lightened as she approached the little house at the end of the block. It was old, the house where her grandfather Wilson had spent most of his life, and it would have been more comfortable with another bedroom at least, but they had a place they could afford. Rents were so high. If her father hadn't inherited the house in South Rutland . . .

Summoning a cheerful smile, Alisa opened the front door. Before she could even get inside, she heard her father's voice. "Hi there, darlin', where've you been? It's about *time* you got home!" But she could hear the smile in his voice and feel the warmth of his welcome, and she was glad to be home in spite of everything.

"Hi, Dad," she responded, placing her books on the sofa and moving to where he was sitting by the reading lamp. She leaned to place a kiss on his forehead, then stood back to look at him. He, too, had managed an attitude of cheer, and she was grateful.

Her father had always been a giant to his family, though he was a physically slight man with thinning blond hair. His real strength, her mother had once said, was in his soul. Bernard Wilson, Alisa thought suddenly as she watched him, was the strongest man she had ever known, and all the Mrs. Carters in the world could never change that.

"What's the matter, Alisa?" he asked her. "You haven't been crying, have you?"

Alisa shook her head and brushed away the tear that she hadn't even been aware of. "Not really," she said. "I was just thinking. I love you, you know that?"

Her father nodded and cleared his throat. "For a scrawny little teenage kid, you're not so bad yourself," he said. "How'd it go today?"

"It was okay," she said, knowing what he had really wanted to ask. "A couple of kids asked me about Mom. They were nice enough. And Mrs. Birnam said if there's anything she can do . . ."

She didn't mention Mrs. Carter, and she didn't mention the people who should have asked but were too uncomfortable with the circumstances to do so.

Again her father nodded. "Most folks are good," he said, "but I know it's hard for you when they ask questions. The best thing is just to tell the truth, though. Meredith will be well again soon, Alisa, and in the meantime we'll all do the best we can."

He's so confident, so sure that everything will turn out all right, Alisa mused as she began preparations for their evening meal. It's remarkable how he can be so accepting, so tolerant of people, without feeling any bitterness even after all that's happened. If I only had his courage . . .

Then she heard the children's footsteps and their chatter and put all musings aside. They would be hungry and eager to tell her about their day at school, and she would have to give them her attention. She couldn't let them see her weakness, her fear of what tomorrow might bring. She *didn't* have her father's courage, but as long as she could manage it, she would keep Marty and Darlene from knowing about her cowardice.

Chapter Two

"SHERRY RICHMOND SAID our mama is crazy," Darlene announced between mouthfuls of baked potato.

A moment of silence prevailed. Then her father, his voice carefully controlled, asked, "What did *you* say, Darlene?"

Darlene brushed the tendrils of dark curls back from her face, and Alisa made another mental note to add to her growing list of things she must do: trim Darlene's hair on Saturday. But she sat still as death while she waited for her little sister's reply.

"I told Sherry that Mama's not crazy, she's just kinda sick," Darlene said. "And then Miss Baker told her not to say anybody's crazy. But Sherry said that *her* mama said our mama's crazy, and then Miss Baker turned the p'jector on and we watched a movie about elephants and stuff in Aferka."

"Af-ri-ca, Darlene; not Aferka," Alisa said automatically.

So it started that early. Even in second grade children were exposed to thoughtless comments from adults and repeated them, innocently heedless of the potential for injury in such remarks. It wasn't fair, yet Alisa could only be grateful that Darlene hadn't seemed distressed, that she had reported the incident in such a matter-of-fact way. Evidently she hadn't been hurt or deeply troubled, and Alisa breathed a deep sigh of relief even as she noted the same relieved expression on her father's face.

What if it had been different? she worried, and her gray eyes darkened as a distressing preview of the possible future flitted through her mind. Darlene would get older and more susceptible and sensitive to emotional pain, and unless their mother recovered completely, both of the younger children would be made to suffer again and again. Wasn't it enough that they had to give up their mother periodically to the locked ward on the fourth floor of St. Luke's Hospital?

Marty reached for his milk and somehow managed to overturn it. When his big blue eyes grew shiny with tears, Alisa bit off the sharp scolding words at the tip of her tongue and made herself smile as she dammed up the spill with her hand.

"Hand me that cracked bowl, Marty," she said. "See, you haven't done any harm. We'll just wipe the milk right off the table into this bowl, then you can set it outside for the cat. I bet she'll be *glad* that you spilled your milk."

"Alisa, you're a wonder," her father said softly when supper was over and the little kids were in bed. "You're so good with Marty and Darlene. Every day I'm grateful for such wonderful children, and especially for you, for making things better for the rest of us.''

''I'm not much of a substitute for Mom, though,'' Alisa replied, feeling somehow ashamed. ''I almost yelled at Marty. Mom never yells at any of us. Not when she's well, I mean.''

''But you *didn't* yell; that's the point,'' her father said. ''You've learned well from your mother's example. Anyway, thank you. I wish we could afford to hire someone; it's too much work for you, with school and housework and the kids. . . .''

''We'll manage, Dad,'' Alisa replied, ''but I do have to study for a math test tonight. I'd better let the dishes go.''

''Get your books. I'll take care of the dishes,'' her father replied. ''And if you have time in the morning, gather up the laundry and I'll do it when I get home tomorrow.''

Alisa nodded. Her father did as much of the housework as he could manage. But every hour spent at such tasks was an hour less for him to use for his studies, and so much depended on that.

She opened her math book and began on the first page of the unit, working and proving sample problems from each newly introduced process. Occasionally she was briefly stumped, but then memory came to her aid. In far less time than she had expected, Alisa had reviewed the whole unit. She would do all right on tomorrow's test.

Her father had finished the dishes and gone to bed, and Alisa sat alone at the table in the quiet house. There was nothing else that had to be done, at least nothing that couldn't wait until Saturday, but she didn't feel sleepy. It would be nice to just sit there for a while. Everything was so quiet and peaceful.

The realization of that thought struck her like a physical blow, and her teeth clenched even as her hand involuntarily crumpled the paper on which she'd been doing the problems. It was *wrong* to enjoy the peacefulness when her laughing, teasing, gentle mother almost certainly lay huddled beneath her shield of protective blankets in a psychiatric ward at that very moment. Guilt for her own disloyal thought overwhelmed her, and her head sank upon her crossed arms on the tabletop.

They had been such a happy family once, without a single real problem. Her father had been an active, busy man with a lively and roving mind. He had worked for an immense plant where airplanes were built; he had even been involved in the government's space program.

Then the plant had been reorganized, and he had lost his position. He could have stayed on at the plant where he had worked since he had completed his second year of college, but he would not have been able to advance or to work in the exciting experimental area of aeronautics that he loved. So the Wilsons had embarked on a drastic venture. After securing a guarantee of being employed again as soon as he was finished, her father had quit work and returned to college—and he had almost earned the degree he needed.

In the meantime they had lived on their savings, and the money was dwindling rapidly because of unexpected problems. But they had moved to her

11

father's childhood home in South Rutland and been able to manage.

At last Alisa raised her head and stood up, moving sluggishly to the refrigerator for a glass of tea. She had gotten tired suddenly—exhausted, in fact—but maybe if she went on, deliberately considering the things that had gone wrong, she might be able to find some relief. Somehow she had to get a better grip on herself. Somehow she had to stop feeling ashamed and angry and afraid and guilty!

At first the new town and the different living conditions had been an adventure. Meredith Wilson had made it that way with her lively imagination and wonderful sense of humor. She had somehow turned every new problem into a challenge. When they discovered that new water pipes had to be installed, carrying water in jugs for three days became an exciting opportunity to learn how their great-grandparents had managed in the days before modern facilities had become common. When they realized that all three kids had to walk clear across town to their schools, their mother persuaded them to think of themselves as explorers, becoming extra observant and learning everything they could about their new environment.

They had barely noticed the new care that had to be taken with expenses, Alisa remembered. Leaving the spacious, gleaming house in the city for the cramped little place in South Rutland where she had to share her bedroom for the first time hadn't been a problem because her mother had made it fun.

Of course it probably hadn't been all that pleasant and easy for her parents, Alisa realized, recalling the few instances when she'd accidentally been allowed glimpses of other moods. There was the day she had slipped quietly in the back door, thinking to surprise her father with the empty birds' nest she had found. She had been surprised when she saw him throw a wrench halfway across the room in an uncharacteristic fit of frustration when he realized that he couldn't fix the water heater and they would have to buy a new one.

Then there was the day she had seen her mother carefully packing her law books into a storage carton. She'd had to drop out of her classes when the expenses had begun to overwhelm them, and she hadn't complained once. "It's only temporary, till Bernard can go back to work," she had insisted. But tears had trickled silently that day as she packed away the books, unaware that Alisa had seen her.

Yes, the changes had been much more difficult for her parents than for their children, Alisa concluded. They had been pretty doggone wonderful, though, putting a bright face on almost everything. And it wasn't that they had simply been pretending for the sake of their children, Alisa felt sure. They were both naturally cheerful and optimistic and didn't easily let life's surprises get them down.

Once in South Rutland, for instance, her mother had gotten to know lots of people, and she had found something to like about everyone she met.

In spite of everything, they'd been doing all right. Then, when they had been in Rutland only a few months, something strange had begun to happen to her mother.

It had begun with what seemed like a simple loss of energy. Then she had grown alternately much quieter, then argumentative and unreasonable, then fearful, until finally she said little and seldom laughed or even smiled. The local doctor had prescribed one thing and another, but nothing helped, and she grew absentminded, letting food burn on the stove and forgetting to do the laundry. Finally she had simply gone to bed and stayed there. She had lacked the will to talk or even eat.

In desperation they had summoned an ambulance, and Meredith Wilson had spent three weeks in the psychiatric ward before she began to improve at last. In another three weeks she was at home again, subdued from the drugs but almost her old self again.

With her mother at home again, Alisa had been able to put aside the terror of her own inadequacy. She had slipped gratefully from beneath the burden of her family's needs and concern for her mother's health and had returned to her regular patterns and interests. Only a few people had even been aware of what had happened; they were still relatively new in town then.

Their medical insurance had paid half the bill. The rest wasn't paid off yet when it happened again.

That time her mother had refused to allow the ambulance attendants to take her to the hospital, and they wouldn't take her against her will. With tears in his eyes, her husband had gone through the necessary legal steps, which required the sheriff to be present when they took her away. As the days passed, Alisa had developed a deep, unexpected revulsion for the brown uniform, the flashing red light, and all the regalia that screamed "sheriff" to all within sight and hearing.

And last night it had happened once more. The doctors said that it was severe depression. It was not simply a case of feeling unhappy and hopeless, but such an intense illness that her mother could not, even with her tremendous willpower, pull herself out of her misery. She *had* to be hospitalized; otherwise, she would have simply starved herself. She'd been deaf to Alisa's pleading, to her efforts to entice her mother back into participation in life.

They had recognized the symptoms for a couple of weeks and had tried to persuade her to enter the hospital on her own.

"I think I'm just run down this time, Bernard," she had insisted. "It isn't the same thing this time, I'm sure. And I do so hate to leave you and the kids. Oh, why can't I get better?"

But she hadn't gotten any better.

Alisa ran her fingers through her short brown hair and got to her feet once more. It was getting late, and she was truly tired now. What good had it done, after all, to go through all the misery again? Nothing had been solved, and the same feeling of guilt and shame burdened her.

The house was quiet and peaceful.

Someone was taking care off her mother.

It was a relief. Wrong or not, it was a relief, and with head bowed and shoulders slumped, Alisa turned off the light and went to her room.

Chapter Three

IT WAS EARLY April, and that meant there were only six more weeks of school. Alisa couldn't help feeling glad of that. It wasn't that she didn't like school. She did, and Rutland High was better than her former city school. It was more personal, she felt, probably because it wasn't so big. In her two years there she had come to know her teachers and most of the students rather well. She knew that the psychology teacher, Mrs. Birnam, lived with her husband in the Pinewoods Subdivision on the north side. And she knew that Mr. Reed was divorced, had no children, and was the legal guardian of a younger brother who attended a midwestern college specializing in graduating engineers. It was nice to feel that her teachers were real and in many ways so ordinary. Still, the end of school meant springtime, and maybe spring would bring other good things with it.

Mr. Reed was awfully likable, she thought as she sat listening to him in seventh-hour English class. The class was supposed to be American literature, but sometimes it seemed more like her idea of a philosophy class. Mr. Reed's teaching was all right, too, but on some days she suspected that he was a bit too intense about his conviction that literature equaled life.

"Literature is like a magic mirror in which those with a maturing vision can see a clear reflection of the soul of mankind," he was saying to the attentive class. "In fact, literature may be the *only* place we can find a true representation of the human spirit. It cannot be seen directly; there are no drawings of the soul; the greatest scientists and philosophers of all time have been unable to say where man's soul, his mind, his spirit *is*. Yet we know it exists, and we can begin to comprehend the magnificence of it all with careful attention to literature."

"Are you saying that we might really understand about such things sometime in the future?" Simon Bunch asked from where he sat behind Alisa. "And if we ever do, will that be good? I've always been told that we weren't *meant* to understand some things."

"Perhaps we aren't," Mr. Reed replied, leaning against his desk and reaching to smooth the back of his gray-streaked wavy hair. "Yet mankind has been blessed—or maybe tormented is more accurate—with the power of thought, by the greed for knowledge, the eagerness to comprehend and explain the mysteries of the universe. Why are we like that, so different from the rest of the animal kingdom, if we weren't meant to find the answers we're searching for so intently?"

"I don't think that's it at all, Mister Reed," Valerie Phillips said from across the room. "I think all of our . . . trying to learn, our continuous exploration, is just a search for adventure. There aren't any more continents to explore, so people are looking for something else, anything new they can find.''

''All right,'' Mr. Reed said. ''Perhaps you're right. But why? Why is there such a need for *adventure*? Why aren't we more easily satisfied? Surely there's something else involved besides adventure for its own sake to explain the need that's driving mankind. What might it be?''

''Boredom,'' an unidentified voice suggested.

''Trying to be happy,'' someone else said.

They're both right, Alisa thought, troubled by the direction the discussion had taken. And maybe Mr. Reed was right, too, since literature was necessarily a recording of people's thoughts and words and actions. Maybe it would be fine to comprehend how the parts of oneself that were so seldom considered actually functioned or how they were supposed to function. Maybe people were just searching for an all-purpose key to existence that would finally give them control of their lives.

She realized that the room had grown quiet, and she glanced up to see Mr. Reed watching her. Had he spoken to her? She didn't know, and she flushed and looked down at her desk.

''Alisa? What's on your mind? What do you think of all this?'' he asked her.

''I think . . . that everyone wants to be happy, more than anything else,'' she replied hesitantly, uncomfortable with the question, ''but we don't know how to . . . to go about the business of *living* well enough. There's a big mystery about it. Happiness . . . how to find it . . . seems to be a secret from all but a few lucky people. Most people think about it constantly in one way or another, but we only experience it in little short moments."

"When we aren't even looking," Sherry Tinsley added almost under her breath. Then, stronger: "And then it's gone before we realize it. We usually don't even know we were happy until we look *back* and see it."

"A fine and honest observation," Mr. Reed said in a soft voice. Alisa didn't know whether he meant her comments or Sherry Tinsley's. It didn't matter.

"Let's assume for a moment that a search for happiness does explain man's restlessness," he went on. "How will we discover it, the secret that Alisa spoke of? Could a hint of the answer to that question possibly be found in literature?"

"Thoreau didn't even mention happiness in our reading assignment for today," Simon replied. He sounded grumpy to Alisa. Simon occasionally complained that the talks in English class rambled around too much. He liked to stick to the subject. Simon trusted *facts*.

"Well, Simon, it's like what we said earlier about man's search for an understanding of his own soul," Mr. Reed said with a twinkle in his eyes. "Happiness can't be defined by talking about it directly, either. Our language is always inadequate that way. We have to look for answers between the lines, so to speak. Just remember, students, that feelings, moods, emotions tend to be infectious. So when you do stumble onto a bit of happiness, spread it around. Try to infect others. And for tonight, I want you to read pages three hundred forty through three hundred sixty-six.''

And that completed Thursday's formal education. As she walked toward home, Alisa wished for a moment that Mr. Reed's class could be earlier in the day instead of the last period. So much of the time, his comments and the response they produced troubled her and remained in her thoughts when it would have been less of a burden to think of other things. But walking home, it was hard not to think about the things she'd just heard.

Happiness! What a subject, not to mention his blasted ''search for comprehension of the human soul,'' or however he had put it. Who could even *think* of such things when there were so many problems and pains, so much drabness and emptiness and frustration? What did the location of the human mind have to do with fixing supper and helping Darlene and Marty with their homework? How could she find the energy to ''read between the lines'' of Thoreau's writing, with housework and worry about her mother and trying not to lose patience?

And yet her father was a happy person. He knew the secret of happiness, and he had never lost sight of it for more than the briefest periods, even with the loss of his job and having to sacrifice the family savings so he could go back to school.

And her mother had once known the secret as well. True, it had slipped away now because of whatever had driven her into that deep depression. But until her illness she, too, had known how to be a happy person.

And Mr. Reed was happy. That was obvious.

So maybe it wasn't impossible, after all. Somehow, some people had some special understanding. Only maybe that understanding was reserved for adults. Maybe it simply wasn't meant for teenagers. Like the legal driving age, maybe it was something one had to grow into, something one had to earn.

Chapter Four

DARLENE HAD LITTLE to say at supper, but Marty filled the gap eagerly. "We planted seeds today," he informed them. "We dug up the dirt ourselves, with spoons, and we put the dirt in our milk boxes and planted seeds."

"Milk boxes?" his father inquired. "What's that?"

Darlene and Alisa laughed, and Darlene explained. "Marty's talking about milk *cartons*, Dad," she said. "I 'member when we did that at my other school. We saved the milk cartons from our snack time and planted beans in them."

Their father nodded solemnly. "I see," he said, giving Marty his full attention. "What kind of seeds did you plant in your milk carton, son?"

Marty's wide blue eyes darkened somehow, and a little crease appeared across the bridge of his cute nose as he thought hard. Then his whole face brightened. "Happy seeds!" he cried. Then, before anyone could respond, he visibly thought it over, and they waited. "It's not happy seeds," he whispered to himself. Then: "Now I know! It was happi*ness* seeds. That's what it was for sure. Happiness seeds.''

What's all this about happiness? Alisa wondered. Is springtime driving everyone a little silly? But she smiled at her little brother's pleasure. Her father also smiled, but he seemed a bit puzzled.

''Happiness seeds, huh?'' he said thoughtfully. ''It certainly sounds like your teacher chose the right sort of seeds, Marty. But when the seeds come up—when the plant starts to grow—what kind of *plant* will it be, I wonder?''

It was as if he wasn't really asking his son the question but only musing. Nevertheless, Marty had the answer.

''It's gonna be a happiness plant,'' he said. ''My teacher said when it starts to grow good, I can bring it home and put it in the ground, after you help me cut the bottom of the milk box off. She said our mom or dad or somebody who's grown up has to help us do that part. But then, when it's in the dirt, it'll grow big, and then it'll get *beans* on it.''

''Marty, that's silly!'' Darlene declared. ''If it's going to grow beans, you must've planted bean seeds. B'sides, there aren't really any happiness seeds, I don't think. Are there, Dad?''

Before her father could respond, Marty's face had taken on the determined expression that meant he wouldn't give in for anything. ''It was *too* happiness seeds!'' he insisted. ''You don't know about seeds at all, Darlene! My teacher said growing things is a happy thing to do, and she said they were happiness seeds, and she *knows*!''

Reaching one hand to silence the argument that

was sure to come from Darlene, Bernard Wilson never took his gaze off his son's face. "I think maybe Marty's teacher does know about seeds," he said softly, "and I think she was very wise to tell you about happiness seeds. Carry the plant home carefully when the time comes, Marty. It will be nice to have a happiness plant growing in our backyard."

It was suddenly very difficult for Alisa to swallow, and she couldn't bear to look at her father. Then the moment passed, and they talked of other things.

Just before they finished the meal, their father said, "I talked to the doctor today, kids." His tone was very matter-of-fact. "He said that your mother is doing better, that she seems to be feeling more calm now. And he's starting a brand-new treatment this time. I'm not quite sure how it works, but Doctor Marshall seems pretty hopeful about it."

"When can we go and visit Mom?" Marty asked with anxious longing in his voice.

"The doctor thinks we should wait a couple more days," his father replied gently. "I can't promise anything, son, but unless the doctor changes his mind, we'll go after the weekend—say, next Monday after school."

"I just wish Mom could stay home all the time," Darlene said wistfully. "It feels funny if she's not here when we come home from school."

"I know, sugar," her father said, "but it won't be for very long. Maybe you and Marty should start planning your surprises now; what do you say?"

"Okay!" Marty said eagerly, brightening at the

prospect of making a welcome-home gift for his mother. "Let's go and look at our stuff, Darlene."

They hurried toward Marty's bedroom, where their supply of paper, glue, crayons, and such was kept. The "surprise" ritual had begun during their mother's first illness. Marty had been only four years old at that time, but he and Darlene had missed their mother terribly. To make the waiting easier, their father had suggested that the children make surprise gifts for her return home. It had proved to be an excellent project, occupying many evening hours in a mood of eager anticipation.

"How'd you do on the math test?" her father asked when Marty and Darlene had left the room.

"Oh, fine. I got ninety-eight percent," Alisa replied absently.

"That's great," he replied, "but you're not exactly thrilled about it, are you? Something on your mind?"

Alisa looked up to see him watching her quizzically, and she smiled. "Nothing much," she said. "I was just thinking about Marty's happiness seeds."

Her father chuckled. "I must write a thank-you letter to his teacher," he said. "That was a marvelous idea. I like teachers to be positive. And Marty seems to be enjoying school, which is awfully important in the first year. Gets them started with a good attitude."

Alisa nodded. "The funny thing is, in Mister Reed's class today, we were talking about happiness," she said, "and I kept thinking about that discussion while I walked home. Then I thought of Mrs. Carter. Dad, people are funny, aren't they?''

"Granted. But how do you mean?''

"Well . . . most people seem happy some of the time, and a few people manage to seem happy practically all the time. Then there are others, like Mrs. Carter. I don't think she's *ever* happy, Dad. Anyway, I wonder if there's any way a person can, uh, *control* those things. I mean . . . how about you? And Mom, when she's well? Do you have any control over how you feel? Do you think that happy people are just lucky, or is it possible that they just *choose* to be happy, at least part of the time?''

"Possibly the latter,'' her father replied, leaning back and rubbing his chin thoughtfully. "I remember once, years ago . . . in a place where I used to work. We had a break room—a room where the workers dropped in a couple of times a day for coffee. Anyway, it got so that I couldn't stand to go in there on my break, because the men were always complaining, always grumbling about something. Thinking back on it, it seems like they had simply fallen into a *habit* of despair. And when I'd stay among them for a few minutes, hearing about so much misery, well, it seemed as if I would feel rotten for the rest of the day.''

"Are you saying that those men were making themselves miserable when they could have been more contented? If that's right, Dad, do you believe that if people just realized what they were doing, like the way Mrs. Carter seems to *focus* on unpleasant things, maybe they could actually change the way they feel?''

26

"That may be exactly right, Alisa," her father replied. "I had never really thought about such a thing until I worked in that place. But while I was there, I did realize that I was pretty strongly influenced by the attitudes of the other men. I decided that if I wanted to feel optimistic, I had to avoid negative things as much as I could."

She considered her father's comment and then looked up at him, searching for words to express the idea trying to take form in her thoughts.

"If you're right, Dad," she said at last, "then it's not all just . . . accidental. Maybe that's what Mister Reed meant today. He said that happiness was infectious. And you've just suggested that despair is, too."

"So how do *you* feel about it?"

"It sure is a nice idea," she mused, "to imagine I could have more influence on the way I feel, that I wouldn't always have to feel so . . . controlled by things I can't change. It's a nice idea."

"But you don't quite believe it yet?" her father inquired gently.

Alisa did not reply. If it was really true. . . . But as badly as she wanted to rid herself of the thoughts that made her feel so bad sometimes, she was old enough to know that wishing wouldn't get her anywhere. No, she couldn't believe it could ever truly work, at least not for her.

Chapter Five

ALISA HAD WALKED only half the fourteen blocks between her house and the school when the first raindrops began to speckle her books and her trim navy jumpsuit. If the real rain would hold off for just two blocks more, she would be in front of the Laundromat, where she could stand inside until it stopped. She remembered having seen a pay phone there; if the rain continued, she'd be able to call a cab.

She had been careless and had forgotten her umbrella, though the heavy gray sky had reminded her to see that Marty and Darlene carried theirs and wore raincoats. Everything seemed to be so rushed in the mornings, no matter how early she got up. It was a wonder she had even remembered her books. If only her mother were well! The mornings used to go so smoothly. Alisa had never felt that the clock was her enemy till now.

Irritated at her own forgetfulness and walking as fast as she could, she was barely aware of the automobile that had slowed beside her until the horn sounded. At that she glanced up, relieved to see Paul Heyser at the wheel. Paul was a junior, too, and moodily attractive; that was about all she knew about him, but at least he wasn't a stranger.

"Want a ride?" he asked with an obvious lack of interest.

With a car like this, she thought after she was comfortably seated next to him, a rainy day should be pure pleasure! It was all gleaming elegance and luxury in Paul's automobile. She had noticed before that the clothes he wore were always in the newest, most casual fashion and carried only the best designer labels. The way such things usually worked in high school, Paul Heyser should have been president of the student council or captain of the football team at the very least. He was certainly smart enough for one and built well enough for the other.

But Paul was neither. As nearly as she was aware, he didn't participate in any of the extracurricular activities. They were in the same math, psychology, and English classes and had shared a couple of classes the year before as well—or the second half, anyway. He had moved to Rutland several months after Alisa's arrival there. In spite of all that, she realized as the silence in the car began to bother her, she had only rarely heard Paul Heyser speak.

She had already thanked him for stopping, to which he had responded with a shrug. Ordinarily she'd never be bothered by silence; rather, she had always treasured the rare times in her life when all was quiet. But in the car with Paul, closed in by the rain that drummed against the windows, she felt uncomfortable as the silence grew.

"How'd you do on the math test yesterday?" she finally asked, desperately trying to change the atmosphere.

"Okay. I got a hundred percent."

"Well," she replied, feeling foolish, "I guess that *was* okay."

He glanced at her, then turned his attention back to his driving. "I didn't mean to sound stuck up. It was easy for me because I already had the same stuff before I came here," he said. "I was in a private school before. As my mother would be all too quick to tell you, it was a very select student body. All 'achievers.' We learned—or else." The dullness in his tone somehow intensified the sarcasm in his choice of words, and Alisa fumbled for a way to respond.

"It must be interesting to go to a private school," she said, thinking even as she spoke how inane her comment sounded. It was always so obvious when a person *worked* at conversation. Everything came out either "interesting" or "fascinating."

"I wish the rain would stop," she said, knowing that her second try wasn't much of an improvement.

"I like the rain," he responded instantly, with sincere feeling in his voice. She was surprised.

"Why?" she asked.

"It's like a . . . curtain," he said. "It hides the ugliness of this place for a little while."

"You don't like Rutland?"

He shrugged. "I heard you're kinda new here, like me," he said. "You must see it, too, the way

30

everything in this part of town is so crummy, the way nobody has any pride.''

But it was *her* part of town he was speaking of, and although his observation hadn't wounded her, she saw that he had recognized his blunder too late. His already dark complexion flushed a deeper shade, and his shoulders slumped.

"Listen, I didn't mean . . . I forgot. Me and my big mouth and my snotty attitude!" He wasn't just regretful; she could hear clearly in the controlled viciousness behind his final words his condemnation of himself. A wave of sympathy swept through her. She wanted nothing more at that instant than to erase that bitterness and make him feel better.

"It's dreary enough, no question about that," she said, even managing a bit of a laugh. "But most towns seem to have a shabby area. It's as predictable as sunrise, isn't it? Tell you what—let's get together sometime and just talk. Maybe we can get over this silly awkwardness."

Amazed at her own nerve, she didn't dare say another word. Maybe, she thought, he would think her forward or flirtatious and never talk to her again. But even if he did, she couldn't regret her invitation. She'd felt that she had to say *something*, and it was the best she'd been able to do.

He was occupied with parking the car then and didn't answer her immediately. When he had removed the ignition key and gotten his literature book from the console, he turned toward her.

"Did you mean that, or were you just trying to make me feel less of a fool?"

"I meant it," she said, "and yes, I was trying

to make you feel better, too.'' Then she grinned at the oddness of it all. ''I hope it worked,'' she said lightly.

''It worked,'' he replied. ''Thanks.''

Chapter Six

SHE SAW HIM in the hallway once, taller and more muscular than most of the other boys, and he gave her a half wave. In psychology and math classes she knew he was there, but there wasn't any real occasion for her greeting. Then, in English class, he took the seat immediately behind her. The seats weren't assigned, but most of the kids kept to the same ones anyway, and Simon had been sitting behind Alisa for months.

Simon Bunch wasn't a nerd, but everything about him seemed to be methodical. Alisa had become aware that Simon was completely predictable. He wore his Bullet Boys T-shirt on Tuesdays, and his notebook was always perfectly ordered; he never had to search through it for his homework.

And now Paul had taken his seat. Simon wasn't known for any reluctance to speak up. What would he do when he saw his seat occupied? It wasn't a big deal, but still, it was the kind of thing Simon wouldn't like.

He came into the room laughing with two other boys, then turned down the aisle toward his accustomed place. He was almost there when he noticed

Paul, and Alisa watched, curious and expectant. But Simon simply looked the situation over for a moment and then took an empty seat in the next row without saying a word.

Mr. Reed entered the room then. Though it was the final period of what must have been a busy day, he appeared fresh and energetic, as usual. He counted heads and quickly identified the single absentee, then reached for the textbook on his desk and opened it to a marked page.

"If you've completed your reading assignment, you will remember this," he said. Then he read a couple of sentences from Henry David Thoreau's essay "Civil Disobedience" and closed the book.

"Thoreau wrote this essay sometime around 1845, when slavery was still being practiced in this country," he said, "and I have two questions for you. First, what is the implication for society in his statement, and second, to what, if any, extent does it apply in this century? Sherry, would you respond to the first question?"

"It seems clear enough," Sherry said after a moment's thought. "He said that *one man* could put an end to slavery. But it doesn't make much sense, because lots of people knew that slavery was wrong and nobody'd been able to stop it."

Mr. Reed nodded. "You've told us what he said, and you've given us your reaction to that," he said, "but you still haven't explained what those words *imply*." He looked over the classroom and selected a raised hand. "Tom?"

"Thoreau meant that any reform movement is started by a single person, that there *has* to be someone to begin it," Tom Jarret said. "I think he was suggesting that once that single man comes forward and takes the first steps, others will join him and carry the movement on until they've accomplished the goal. But nothing can happen until that single man does something."

"So in one sense things like that really *are* done by one man," Larry Wunderlich added. "It's sort of a weird way of saying it, but when you look at it like Thoreau did, it does make sense, doesn't it?"

It's always like this in Mr. Reed's class, Alisa thought, seeing him smile and nod to someone else who wanted to speak. For some reason, most of the kids were eager to offer their ideas or ask questions. Even when their answers were as wrong as could be, Mr. Reed never made them feel ignorant. At the same time, he had a painless way of taking what seemed at first like a perfect response and picking it to pieces until they couldn't help recognizing the flaws and seeing a clearer picture.

She heard the lively discussion that followed even as another part of her mind wandered, and she was ready to respond when Mr. Reed addressed his second question to her: "To what, if any, extent does Thoreau's statement apply in this century?"

"In a way it's still true, of course," she said with confidence, "but our society is so much more complicated than it was when he was living. It seems to me that it's a lot more difficult for one person's voice to be heard. That's probably why so many people don't even try to change anything. They think it's hopeless."

"*Is* it hopeless, though?" Mr. Reed asked. "How about it, Paul? I think we can agree with Alisa's observations as far as they go, but what do you think? *Is* it still possible for one person to make a significant change in his society?'"

"It's possible," Paul replied quietly, "but only if that person is rich and influential in politics or big business or something. He'd have to be pretty powerful."

"I disagree," Mr. Reed said. The class was surprised at his bluntness; everything grew quiet while they watched Mr. Reed.

He allowed the silence to continue for a moment. Then he said, "I have an idea how we might test Thoreau's position. We could try it and find out. Anybody interested?"

Again the room was quiet as the students looked at one another with shrugs and raised eyebrows. Mr. Reed waited without movement or expression until someone finally said, "What do you mean, Mr. Reed?"

"Identify a problem and see if you can't bring about a solution," he said, as if they were discussing something simple. "What troubles you? What irritates you? What do you complain about? Just keep this in mind: Before you try to change anything, study it from every angle. You can't solve a problem effectively until you understand the factors that have created the problem in the first place. I would like all of you to give this some thought during the weekend and see whether there isn't something you would like to attempt."

"But what can *we* do?" someone protested.

"Teenagers don't have any influence. We aren't allowed to make any important decisions."

"Baloney!" Mr. Reed said. "I realize that it would take a lot more time than we have for one of you to influence foreign policy or reorganize the social security program. But during the next six weeks you *can* do something worthwhile if you decide that you actually want to. Of course you'll want to use common sense. If you're taller than you'd like to be, you can't make yourself shorter unless you're anxious to cut your feet off, and you can't change anyone else, either. But you might very well cause someone else to want to change *himself*. So give it some thought and tell me on Monday whether you've identified a problem and think it's worthwhile to look for a solution."

"Will we get a grade for this?" someone asked.

Mr. Reed frowned at the speaker, clearly displeased. "If you're asking whether you *have* to do this, the answer is no," he said. "I offer this to inquisitive, potentially productive students as a challenge. If there's any discussion of grading to be done, *I'll* bring it up."

"Now," he went on in a more pleasant tone, "give it some thought, and on Monday we will see whether there's anything to talk further about."

Alisa was aware that Paul had followed her out of the classroom, and he stopped beside her at her locker.

"The stuff I told you this morning about the easy math test and the private school I went to," he said, shifting his books awkwardly, "sure doesn't apply to Reed's class. He won't leave us alone for a minute!''

"What do you mean?" Alisa asked, closing her locker door and turning to face him.

"It's just . . . all these odd things he brings up. What could he possibly expect *us* to do?'''

"I don't know, either," she said thoughtfully, "but it's an intriguing idea. I sort of started thinking about a project while he was talking, but I *know* it's not possible. And besides, I don't have time right now to hardly even think about it. But I wish . . .''

"What?" he prompted her when she didn't finish the sentence.

"Oh, it's too silly to mention," she said. "It's about this whole town, practically. And you can't change a town.''

"Come on, tell me," he urged. He smiled then, and the rigid planes of his face relaxed. For a moment all she could think of was how handsome Paul became when he smiled.

"I . . . look, I'll tell you, but not now," she said, suddenly noticing that the hallway had already emptied. "I have to get home. My . . . my mother's in the hospital, and I have a little brother and sister.''

"Would it be all right if I drove you home?" he asked, and it seemed odd that such an attractive boy, obviously from a well-to-do family, would seem hesitant about such a thing.

"Well . . . sure, I guess so," she replied. "I don't think Dad will mind. Thanks, Paul.''

In his car he urged her once more to explain her idea. Feeling a bit foolish, she began.

"This town is almost like *two* towns," she said. "There's South Rutland, where I live, and the rest of the town is usually just called Rutland. I understand the main difference: the poor people live in South Rutland. And that's the problem—not that we're poor, but the other thing you said this morning. That it's so dreary there, that hardly anybody on that side of town appears to have any pride, any concern for how their community looks."

"Listen," he said haltingly, "I'm sorry about that. It was a stupid thing. I wish I hadn't—"

"No, please," she protested. "It wasn't just that you said it, honestly. That didn't bother me. See, I've been thinking about it a lot lately, how life is sometimes so full of troubles, and people sort of get into a hopeless way of not caring, of just . . . accepting whatever happens and not trying to change their lives. Anyway, my dad seems to think part of it is just a habit, and habits can be changed. So that's why I thought about it in Mister Reed's class—because I've been talking to Dad about things like that. And I just wished for a minute that there could be a way to make the people in South Rutland have more interest in the appearance of their town. But it's impossible, of course. Remember, I told you it was silly."

He nodded thoughtfully as though agreeing. Then he said, "I can't figure it out. I've never been interested . . . I never have believed in much of anything. I just tried not to see what I figured I couldn't change. And I *know* that people are cruel and stu-

39

pid. There're idiots everywhere you look! But Mister Reed's been getting to me, and since this morning you, maybe. I guess I'm getting soft in the head! I almost believe it *is* possible to do something useful. I wonder what Mister Reed would say about you and me working as a team—I mean, if you'd maybe want to.''

"Gosh, I don't know," Alisa replied, overwhelmed. "I don't think Mister Reed would mind, and it would be okay with me, but . . . are you talking about my idea? About South Rutland?''

"It might not be a bad idea," he said. "We could at least think about it, couldn't we? I mean, maybe we could do *something*.''

"Okay, I'll think about it," Alisa finally conceded, "but I'm telling you right now, Paul, we'd be setting ourselves up for a big disappointment. The stuff Mister Reed and my dad say *sounds* good, but it seems an awful lot like believing in fairy tales to me.''

Chapter Seven

Friday evening passed quietly. Marty reported that his happiness seed, which had been planted only two days, *still* hadn't done anything except lie there in the dirt. And Darlene complained that reading was becoming too difficult, insisting that she had decided she didn't want to read, after all, and wasn't going to do it anymore no matter *what* Miss Baker said. But after a little while, Marty had forgotten his disillusionment and Darlene struggled with the writing on the peanut butter jar until she had figured most of it out.

Alisa washed the dishes and made a grocery list with her father's help, then they all watched a western movie. Marty fell asleep on the sofa with his feet in Alisa's lap, and she carried him to bed when the movie was over. It wasn't an exciting evening, but sometimes it was nice to do nothing important for a little while.

Once in bed, though, Alisa found her thoughts turning to the events of the day. Paul was nice, and apparently he didn't fit any of the common stereotypes about rich boys. He was even a bit bashful and not exactly confident in spite of his good looks, his intelligence, and the terrific car and clothes and everything. The morning rain had been a good thing, after all; because of it, she had gotten to know Paul a little bit.

But the other thing—Mr. Reed's suggestion—was just a bit too much, she thought. Maybe if her mother wasn't ill and she didn't have to stay so busy at home all the time . . . Only that kind of thinking was definitely pointless. She would hate to tell Paul on Monday to forget the whole thing, but wasn't it the only sensible thing to do? She certainly didn't need any more disappointments or responsibilities, and trying to do something that was sure to result in failure wouldn't exactly help improve her morale, either.

The morning dawned soft and warm and sunny, and as soon as they'd had breakfast, Darlene and Marty ran for the backyard. Alisa cleaned up their breakfast things and began gathering the small rugs to take them outside and shake them out. Her father, reading in the living room, called her to him.

"I don't want you doing any heavy cleaning this weekend," he said firmly. "Take it easy, Alisa. Relax, read, or . . . is there somewhere you'd like to go?"

"I appreciate your thoughtfulness, Dad," Alisa said, laying the rugs aside and dropping into a chair, "but it's pretty bad here. The house hasn't been really cleaned for a couple of weeks. And I don't have anything special to do, anyway."

"Just the same, I want you to loaf a little bit," he said. "You're busy every evening, and that's enough. I've found someone to come in once a week and do the big jobs. She'll be here on Monday.''

''But Dad, we can't afford that,'' Alisa protested. ''I admit it would be nice, but . . .''

''Depends on priorities, whether or not we can afford it,'' her father replied. ''We can't afford to move into one of those elegant places on the other side of town, but I've decided that we *can* afford a cleaning woman once a week.''

His remark about the other side of town brought a frown to Alisa's features, and her father said, ''What's the matter? Don't you trust your old man to handle this family's finances?''

''Oh, don't be silly; it's nothing like that,'' Alisa said. ''You just reminded me of something that happened in Mister Reed's class yesterday. Another one of his goofy ideas.''

Then she had to tell him the whole thing, of course, and as she might have expected, he didn't see anything goofy about any of it.

''He's right, you know,'' her father said. ''You should try it; you can figure it out. And the boy, Paul—if he's anything like his father, he's smart enough at least.''

''You know Paul's father?'' she asked, surprised and curious.

''Sure,'' her father said. ''We grew up together. You see, Alisa, South Rutland wasn't always so run-down and shabby. This was a pretty nice area when I was a kid. And Paul's father— he lived on the north side even then, but we were friends. There wasn't all that much difference then.''

But she was interested in the present. "Tell me about him," she urged "What is Paul's family like?''

"Ha, you want gossip, I see," her father teased. "Well, I refuse to indulge you. I'll tell you a few facts and that's all. Paul's father is John Heyser; he's a successful building contractor, and he lives near Chicago, though he might be working practically anywhere. Paul's his only child, and John and his wife are divorced now. Paul spends summers with him. And that's all you'll get from me.''

"Oh, Dad, you're terrible," she groaned. "I'm just curious. I'd never talked to Paul until yesterday; he seemed nice but a little bit . . . unhappy, I guess. Moody.''

"He probably is nice," her father said. "His folks are okay; at least there's nothing glaringly wrong with them. As for the unhappy part, I wouldn't know. His mother used to be a little high and mighty; she may be hard to live with—uh, oh, you tricked me after all!'' he said. "Enough on that subject!''

"All right," she said, laughing, "but what do you think about the other thing, my harebrained idea? According to Mister Reed, we have to understand the causes of a problem before we can try to solve it. The problem is that this side of town is shabby and dreary and awful. Paul said the cause is that the people don't have enough pride, and I agree. What do you say?''

"Could be," her father agreed. "And the reason for that? In my opinion, it starts with a feeling of hopelessness, and the hopelessness becomes a way of life for some people."

"So how can anyone alter that?" she asked. "Surely that must be something that people have to do for themselves if it's to be done at all."

"Of course," her father said, "and that would require a struggle. For many, it would be a tremendous effort, as your teacher said. But while you can't *make* people feel differently, it should be possible to inspire them to want to, at least."

"How?"

"Provide them with an attractive goal, something that's within their power to achieve. Maybe even tantalize them with a reward."

"Dad, what I've got in mind is simple enough," she said. "All I'm thinking about is getting people to clean up their yards, maybe fix up their houses a little bit—just plain clean up this side of town. Imagine how much better this block where we live would look, Dad. Just visualizing that ought to be inspiration enough for anyone!"

"Yes, the satisfaction should be a fine reward," he said, "and it's worth trying. But Alisa, *everybody* resists change. When you've been in a pattern for a long time, it's *hard* to make a change. You might find that you'll have to offer something tangible just to get people interested."

"But what could Paul and I do?" she cried. "We're just a couple of teenagers. It would be miracle enough if anyone even listened to us, much less our coming up with rewards!"

"Oh, I'm sure you'll think of something," her father replied, smiling. "That is, if you decide that you really want to."

Chapter Eight

Freedom from the heavy cleaning was a pleasure, especially since it had been so unexpected. The trouble was that after they'd had lunch, Alisa couldn't think of anything she wanted to do. It would be pleasant to just hide out in her room and read for a while, she thought. She had just started a new novel a couple of days ago. But it was so nice and warm outside that it seemed a shame to remain indoors. Later in the evening it would probably get kind of chilly; maybe she would read then.

"I think I'll go for a walk," she said when the lunch things had been cleared away.

"Me, too!" Marty cried, jumping up, and Darlene looked expectantly at her big sister, too.

"Not this time, kids," their father said. "I'd like to go out to the backyard and play some catch. If you guys go with Alisa, who'll I play with?"

Playing catch with their father was even more attractive than walking with Alisa, and she felt grateful to him for thinking of it. She didn't mind being with Marty and Darlene, of course. How could she? They were her family, and she loved them.

It was funny the way *everything* was so different with their mother away. Under normal conditions, Alisa considered, she'd think nothing of saying to her brother and sister, "Go outside and play and leave me alone!" But although nobody had even once told her that she had to treat them differently while their mother was ill, she had found that it came naturally most of the time. While she had no difficulty refusing them things that wouldn't be good for them, such as snacks before meals, it wasn't at all easy to say no to their innocent and harmless requests even when it made things more difficult for her.

But her father had intercepted them. He didn't have classes during the weekends. He would enjoy taking a break from the books, being outside and playing with the kids—and she would have the afternoon to herself.

Still, where would she go? Half a block from her house she paused and turned around, just looking. Theirs was a neat white frame house with a gabled roof and a carport on the left side. A roofed but unscreened porch extended all the way across the front of the house, and a vining rosebush covered the framework of the porch. Soon it would bloom.

It was a nice place without being at all impressive, except in contrast to the houses on either side. The one on the left appeared diseased, scabby with flaking paint and ragged screens. The house on the right wasn't so bad in itself, but an old car with flattened tires and no hood sat rotting in the front yard. In the backyard, though she couldn't see it from where she stood, Alisa knew there were three other empty shells of discarded automobiles. And the backyard would soon be waist-deep in weeds if last summer's pattern continued.

Down the street from the diseased house were two more houses where everything was reasonably neat. Children's toys, two tricycles, a red wagon, and something that looked like a giant yellow worm with a steering wheel and pedals cluttered one front porch, but there wasn't really anything wrong with that.

In the adjoining lot there was no house at all, or at least not an inhabited one. The lot was a jungle, with several summers of unhampered growth surrounding a dilapidated shed. Loosened sheets of the tin roof rattled in the breeze. A faded "Lot for Sale" sign hung from one corner on the shack, but the sign had been there for at least a year. "I wish we could buy that lot," her mother had said once, "just so we could clean it up."

Then she passed a whole block of poor but cared-for homes, and she waved to Tracey Rogers, a sophomore at Rutland High who was pushing a lawn mower and working on an early tan, wearing shorts and a narrow halter top.

Then there was Mrs. Carter's house, and Alisa could already see the woman sitting in her chair on the front porch, just as she always did.

"Mrs. Carter is lonely; she hasn't any children, and I don't think anyone ever visits her," Meredith Wilson had said. "I think she would be a lot healthier if she just had someone to pay a little attention, to care about her." And when she was well, she

49

had made a point of stopping to talk to Mrs. Carter a couple of times each week.

Should *she* stop and visit? Alisa wondered. She didn't like talking to Mrs. Carter, but remembering her mother's unfailing kindness and compassion, she slowed her steps as she approached the woman's yard.

"Hello, Mrs. Carter," she said, making her tone light and friendly. "How are you today?" Uh-oh, I shouldn't have said that, she thought; she'll be sure to tell me.

The woman didn't disappoint her. "Well, now, I'm not feeling too good, to tell the truth," she complained. "I reckon it was that rain yesterday, got my arthritis all stirred up. But like I always say, everybody's got troubles. How's your mama doing? I sure do miss her dropping by now 'n' again."

"Dad talked to her doctor. He says she's improving," Alisa replied. "It looks as though we'll get to visit soon, maybe Monday, Dad thinks."

"That's good news," Mrs. Carter said, nodding her head vigorously. "You tell her I'm thinkin' about her and prayin' she'll get well real soon, you hear?"

"I'll be sure to do that," Alisa said. Then, without knowing she was going to say such a thing, she went on. "Mrs. Carter, it's springtime. Wouldn't it be nice if we could sort of clean up this neighborhood? Maybe plant some flowers or something?"

"Clean it up? Why, what do you mean, girl?"

"Well, just do some things to make it look better, more cheerful," Alisa replied, fumbling for words. Whatever had possessed her to bring up such a thing, anyway? she wondered, especially to this woman!

Mrs. Carter stared at her as though she'd suggested painting every house on the block purple. Then she turned and slowly gazed about her, toward the adjacent homes and those across the street, as though she hadn't seen them lately. Finally her gaze settled on Alisa once more.

"I reckon the neighborhood could use a little cleanin' up at that," she said, "but who'd do it? *I* can't do much of anything, what with my arthritis and all. It'd be a lot of work. Who'd do all that work?"

"Why, the people who live here, of course," Alisa said, surprised. "The people who own the property."

"Well, now, some of us own our own places, all right," Mrs. Carter said. "And then some of 'em are rent houses that belong to them ritzy folks over in Rutland. I don't know how the folks who're rentin' would take to doing much work on places that don't belong to 'em. Then, too, there's always a lot of good-for-nothing shiftless folk. *They* don't care nothing for flowers and such. Why, you couldn't move some folks with a bulldozer!"

So much for her grand idea, Alisa thought as she walked on after she'd finally escaped from Mrs. Carter. She hadn't thought of the business about rental houses, and she hadn't even considered that people might not even *care*, as Mrs. Carter had suggested. Her steps lagged, and she felt tired; it didn't seem so warm and springlike anymore.

Everything was suddenly so depressing. All along she'd been *saying* that the idea could never work, that it was just a silly notion. But somewhere inside herself she must have actually been thinking that maybe it was possible. Otherwise she wouldn't have this heavy sense of disappointment. Mrs. Carter had thrown cold water on her little try at enthusiasm.

She walked on, no longer paying so much attention to her surroundings, until she came to the busiest street in South Rutland, where several inelegant places of business showed a little Saturday afternoon activity. There she turned to retrace her steps. She would go back and read, after all. If she encountered desolation in her reading, at least she would know it was fictional. She would take the shortest way back home, too, even though she'd have to pass Mrs. Carter's house again. She would simply wave and maybe say hello and keep on walking.

But it wasn't that simple. "Hey there, girl, stop 'n' talk a minute," Mrs. Carter called from her porch.

"I really don't have time right now," Alisa replied. "I have things to do at home."

"I've been thinkin' about what you said a while ago," Mrs. Carter interrupted, "and it'd be right nice if I could have me a couple of them azalea bushes out here in front, by the side of the walk. I saw some at that nursery on Ninth Street last week when the bus took me to the senior citizens center. Do you suppose they're very expensive? I couldn't afford very much."

"Why . . . I don't know, Mrs. Carter," Alisa replied with surprise. "Tell you what, though. I could stop by on my way home from school on Monday and find out. And maybe if they're not too expensive, I could get a couple for you if you like."

"That would be fine. That'd be right neighborly," Mrs. Carter said with a real smile lighting her ponderous features. "I couldn't afford to spend more'n, say, twelve or fifteen dollars. But there were some mighty pretty ones there, all bloomed out in bright colors. I especially liked the lavender ones. Made me feel better just lookin' at them as we passed by."

Maybe she would bake a cake when she got home instead of reading, Alisa thought as she resumed her walk with a lighter step. Marty and Darlene would like that. They hadn't had a nice home-baked cake in quite a while.

Chapter Nine

THEY HADN'T DONE the grocery shopping yet, and Alisa had already started mixing the cake when she discovered there was only one egg in the refrigerator. The recipe listed three. When she mentioned it, Marty's face fell.

"You can't make us a cake, then," he wailed. "I wanted a cake so *bad*." Judging by his mournful expression, his heart was surely broken.

"We'll have our cake, Marty," Alisa assured him. "The cake doesn't absolutely have to have three eggs in it just because the directions say so. We'll just make up our own directions and use one egg."

At that he brightened. "Could you change it to a chocolate cake, too, instead of an old yellow one?" he asked hopefully. "Chocolate cake's my very best favorite kind!"

"Well . . . let me look at the chocolate cake recipe," she said. "I've already started the yellow cake, but who knows? Maybe I can still add chocolate."

She studied both recipes and decided that she should be able to switch, but she wasn't certain.

"Okay, Marty," she finally said, "tell you what we'll do. We'll try changing it to chocolate, but I don't know all that much about baking. Maybe it won't come out right. And if it doesn't taste good, you mustn't be disappointed, because we can get the right things at the store after supper, and more eggs and everything, and make another cake just the way the directions say."

"Okay," Marty agreed, "I *guess* I could wait till after supper. If I *had* to." But his manner clearly indicated that he had complete faith in his sister's ability to mix the recipes and still produce a delicious cake.

He and Darlene watched every step of the mixing, and they didn't lose interest while they waited for it to come out of the oven. Their father watched the news on television, then came to the kitchen to join them. When Alisa described the process of substitution she had used, he was amused.

"It'll be that way all your life, you know," he remarked.

"Dad, I do not plan to spend a great deal of the rest of my life baking cakes," Alisa responded. "I'm going to be a lawyer, like Mom."

"Maybe the two of you'll go into practice together someday," her father said. He could have been serious or teasing; she couldn't tell which.

"I just hope Mom will be able to go back to school sometime," Alisa said. "She loved it so much." She stopped, regretting that she'd said such a thing, since her mother had dropped out of classes primarily because of her husband's need to get a degree. But if he was disturbed, he gave no sign.

"She'll go back," her father replied firmly. "I'm getting closer; before we know it, I'll be finished and we'll have our old life back. I feel sure of that. We'll move back to the city if she wants, where she'll be close to the university again."

It seemed an odd time to discuss the subject, with she and her father at the kitchen table and Darlene and Marty sitting on the floor in front of the glass door of the oven. But the mood seemed right, and Alisa decided to bring up a question that had nagged at her since the signs of her mother's present depression had become apparent.

"Dad . . . the other two times Mom was sick, the doctor talked as if the depression was completely emotional, that it was caused by . . . well, all the changes she had to make and worry about your work and all that. But Mom never believed it."

Her father nodded his agreement. "Alisa, I'm convinced that Meredith was right," he said. "She's never been the kind of person who could be defeated by hard times, although I do realize that's not exactly something everyone can control. But she has always been optimistic; it's in her basic character to find the bright side of things. That's why I'm so hopeful about Doctor Marshall's different approach this time. I think—at least I hope—that he's got the right idea now."

Alisa felt encouraged by her father's attitude. She, too, had felt that her mother's illness was at least as much organic as emotional. Maybe she could really be cured this time. Then she remembered Mrs. Carter's interest in planting flowers and told her father about it.

"That sounds nice," he said. "Since I'll be home early Monday, why don't I pick you up from school, and we can stop at the flower shop and check on the prices. If they're affordable, we'll simply deliver them to her. Your mother has always said that Mrs. Carter would feel better for a little friendliness."

Alisa agreed. "It was quite a surprise that she was eager to get flowers for her yard," she said. "Now if she'd just clean up that awful, junk-filled front porch."

"One step at a time, Alisa," her father advised. "Perhaps a couple of flowering bushes will brighten her general outlook and she'll decide to take another step in the same direction. Then, who knows . . . maybe her neighbors will get inspired with some of that color and cheer and decide to do something for themselves as well."

Alisa couldn't help laughing at his optimism. "The way you always expect the best, Dad . . . that's one of the things I admire about you. I wish I could be that way. But sometimes it does seem to me that you're not very realistic. Are you?"

"Why not?" her father countered. "You said yourself that everybody's searching for ways to be happy. And flowers bring life and color and variety to our attention, purely for pleasure. That *has* to produce at least a moment of happiness, Alisa, so it's not unrealistic to imagine that people who experience a little taste might reach out for more."

"I'm beginning to understand what Mom means

when she says you're a hopeless romantic," Alisa said. "But I suppose you *could* be right. It's a pleasant thought, anyway."

"No, it's not romanticism," he insisted. "It's common sense. Who wans to be unhappy? Everyone isn't born knowing this, but sooner or later the fortunate ones of us come to understand it: Happiness isn't something that happens accidentally. It's created, Alisa; it's just like your cake there in the oven. It's made, as they say, from scratch. And you didn't have all the ingredients that you thought were required, but look at it, how it's getting so fluffy and golden. You made the cake with the materials that were available. And *that's* what you need to discover for yourself, that happiness occurs in the same way. You make it yourself from whatever materials happen to be at your disposal!"

"And maybe it just takes a little push to get it started, huh? Like seeing flowers in someone else's yard and wanting to find some for your own? That's an awfully simple explanation, Dad!"

"It *is* simple," he replied softly. "It's as simple as . . . love."

Chapter Ten

SHE DIDN'T WANT to think about things that had no explanations. Still, her father's words and her own bothersome curiosity about Mr. Reed's theories remained in the recesses of her mind while they had a slice of the cake, which came out pretty good after all, and then went to the store for groceries. Her father had given his own sort of explanation for some of the things she had wondered aloud about, but his explanation was too simple to be real. Both her parents had that approach to life's surprises, though: the don't-get-excited, take-it-easy way.

One Saturday morning not long after they had come to South Rutland, Darlene, just out of kindergarten, had decided to give herself a haircut. She had come out of the bedroom with tears streaming from wide, frightened eyes and an almost bald spot right in front. Alisa had gasped in shock to see it, but her mother had simply looked the situation over quite calmly while Darlene's tears flowed.

Then she had led Darlene to the hall mirror, and

together they had looked at the awful mess of the child's hair.

"Do you think you should cut your own hair anymore?" her mother had asked, and Darlene had shaken her head, gulping and trying to quit sobbing.

"All right," her mother had said, taking the scissors from her daughter's hand, "let's go into the bathroom, and I'll see what I can do to fix this. And Darlene—I'm going to expect that you won't cut your own hair again until you're all grown up, okay?"

A bit of trimming here and there, combined with the creative use of a curling iron, had covered the bald spot most of the time until the chopped-off part had grown out again. And except for Darlene's refusal to use scissors even to cut paper for a few days, there'd been no unpleasantness at all—no anger, no guilt, no blame, no punishment.

"Why make an issue of such a thing?" her mother had said a few days later when Alisia mentioned it. "In a couple of weeks we'll all have forgotten it. But Darlene won't do it again."

Darlene *hadn't* done it again, but what secret had her mother possessed that had made her so certain? Wouldn't any other mother have at the very least forbidden her child the use of scissors, just for insurance?

At the supermarket Alisa went inside to do the shopping, taking her little sister with her while their father waited in the car with Marty. She found it difficult to keep her mind on her task if both children accompanied her, but it was no problem with one, so they had learned to take turns.

She selected the things that were on her list, but when Darlene saw the seafood department, she tugged at Alisa's sleeve. "Let's get some fish," she said. "You can make the kind Mama makes, can't you? The boiled fish?"

"Broiled," Alisa murmured, "not boiled. *Broiled*. I don't know, Darlene. I've never tried it, and I'm not sure how Mama does it." But just the thought of the flaky delicious fish in hot butter sauce made her mouth water, and she looked at the different kinds of fish uncertainly. If she'd only paid more attention to the way her mother did things . . .

The boy in an immaculate apron behind the display case waited without speaking, and finally Alisa looked up at him. "I'd like to broil some fish," she said, "but I don't know which kind to get. Can you tell me?"

The boy, surely no more than eighteen, flushed and shook his head. "The regular seafood man isn't here," he said, "and I don't know much about this stuff. I'm just filling in this evening. He'll be back tomorrow, though," he added encouragingly.

Disappointed, Alisa started to move away, when a familiar voice stopped her. She turned to find Mr. Reed smiling at her. "You'll want this kind, Alisa," he said, indicating the thick pink slices on the crushed ice. "Have you broiled fish before?"

Alisa shook her head, feeling awkward and embarrassed.

"Then you'll want . . . let's see, there's your fa-

ther and you and your brother and sister, right?"
His forehead wrinkled as he considered.

Again she nodded, and Mr. Reed told the boy
how much of the fish he should wrap.

"Take this little packet of seasonings, too," he
said. "It'll be much simpler, and it's a perfect mix.
It's what I use."

Then, while the boy weighed and wrapped the
fish, Mr. Reed told her how to prepare it, using
such simple, precise directions that she surely
couldn't fail. But how odd for her English teacher
to be helping her in such a way!

"Thank you, Mister Reed," she said while Darlene watched the exchange, silent and interested.
"I'm afraid I'm not much of a cook, but the fish
looked so good."

"Oh, you'll do fine," he said. "Just follow those
directions and you'll have no trouble at all. And
I'm on my way home; if you should forget something, just give me a call."

Then he rolled his cart past them, reaching out
to touch Darlene's curls briefly as he passed. Alisa
watched his tall, lean frame until he turned down
another aisle and was out of sight.

"Who was that man, Alisa?" Darlene asked her.
"He sure was a nice man, wasn't he?"

"Yes, he's a nice man," Alisa replied. "That was
Mister Reed, Darlene. He's my English teacher."

At that Darlene stopped walking to look up at
her in astonishment. "He's your *teacher*?" she
asked, incredulous. "But . . . I didn't know a
teacher could make boiled fish!"

"It's *broiled*, Darlene," Alisa said. And as they

made their way to the checkout lane, she had Darlene say the word correctly a couple of times and gave her a simple explanation of the difference between the two methods of cooking so that she would remember the proper term. But while the girl at the cash register totaled the prices, Alisa smiled at her own musings. Darlene would be surprised, she thought, if she knew how closely her own amazement resembled that of her sister.

Soon they were at home with the groceries put away. Alisa wrote out the directions Mr. Reed had given her, then compared them to a recipe she finally located. They were almost exactly the same, but it was still a good thing that she had listened to Mr. Reed. His instructions were simple and easy to understand. Without them, she doubted that she would have been able to prepare the fish correctly. Some of the instructions in the cookbook didn't make a lot of sense by themselves. Whoever had written the cookbook had used a lot of confusing and vague terms. Mr. Reed had made it easy.

Supper would be later than usual, but since she'd broken her own rule and served the cake earlier, it wouldn't matter. And when he noticed the delicate aroma of the cooking fish, her father came into the kitchen to see what she was doing.

"I thought we were having hamburgers," he said, sniffing with appreciation. "That certainly smells better, though. I'm surprised that you're trying it."

Then she told him what had happened in the supermarket, and he laughed at Darlene's limited perception of teachers' abilities. "Mister Reed is clearly a man who enjoys food,'' he remarked. ''I understand that he's a bachelor, so of course he'd know something about cooking. But broiled fish? To tell the truth, I'm a little surprised myself. And that's not reasonable, of course. Funny, isn't it, the way we tend to put everyone into some familiar category that suits our perception of what they're like?''

''But you don't often do that,'' Alisa said. ''I think you're more . . . fair, or objective maybe, than most people.''

''Still, we're all susceptible,'' her father observed. ''No matter how careful we try to be, we're still likely to stereotype people. Rich kids are spoiled; so is an only child. According to our stereotypes, that's the only possibility. Men don't cook unless they get paid for it.''

''Except at a barbecue grill,'' Alisa added, laughing at how silly and narrow-minded it all sounded when she thought about it deliberately.

''Fat people are jolly,'' her father went on, ''and people with small, squinty eyes are criminals.''

And if someone in your family is in a psychiatric ward, people act like it's something to be ashamed of, Alisa thought against her will. But if you catch *yourself* feeling that way for a minute even though you know better, you feel guilty because you've had disloyal thoughts about someone you love. And while that person you've been so worried about but couldn't figure out how to help by yourself is in the hospital and out of your immediate sight and you know they're being cared for, it's a great big relief. And when you feel relief for something like that, you feel guilty again.

The fish was flaky and perfectly seasoned and delicious. Everyone said it was almost as good as her mother's, but Alisa knew that wasn't true. She didn't want it to be true, anyway.

Some things just shouldn't happen, but terrible things happened just the same to people who were good and kind and gentle and deserved only the best. There wasn't any explanation, and there wasn't any sense or reason to it. What was the point in even trying to make things any better when everything one worked for could be snatched away without even a warning to give a person a chance to brace herself?

Chapter Eleven

ON SUNDAY MORNING Alisa awoke early but didn't want to get out of bed. Her sleep had been restless and filled with disturbing dreams that she could no longer recall, and her neck and shoulders ached. If she could only go back to sleep, maybe remain asleep all day long, perhaps something would have magically changed and she wouldn't feel this overwhelming heaviness.

Then she heard a soft noise, bare feet padding across the floor, and she felt her covers being lifted as Darlene slipped into her bed, trying not to wake her. In another moment her sister's slight frame was snuggled against her back, warm and comforting, and she heard a tiny sigh of contentment from behind her. Marty wasn't like his sister when it came to sleeping. He never seemed to awaken once he'd gone to bed. He slept peacefully every night. But not Darlene.

Giving no sign that she was already awake, Alisa lay there thinking of the countless times Darlene had done the same thing, slipping noiselessly into her sister's bed for warmth and comfort. How many times had she awakened to find that thin little body by her side, sometimes deeply asleep, sometimes wakeful but still and silent? Even when they had lived in the city and all was well, Darlene had crawled into her bed occasionally, though it had happened more frequently during the times when their mother was not with them.

She was always so careful not to disturb her big sister, but Darlene's getting into her bed was one thing Alisa never minded. Oh, there were other things, of course, things Darlene and Marty did that irritated her, that made her boil with frustration and resentment. Marty couldn't stand to see Alisa reading contentedly. If he found her reading, there were suddenly a hundred questions that he wanted answers to, and most of them began with the impossible "Why?" And he would not be put off, would not be distracted by threats or promises, and sometimes she couldn't keep herself from yelling at him.

Darlene especially loved to pick through the things on her dresser, the cologne and jewelry and makeup that she had placed just where she wanted them and that Darlene was sure to disarrange or spill or drop onto the floor. She, too, asked questions, innumerable questions. They were not of the same sort as Marty's, but in their own way they were often more difficult, since they dealt with real issues and people and situations.

"Why does Joey Marshall steal everybody's pencils?"

"How come you keep so many books, when you've already read them all?"

"Why can't the doctor make Mama get well?"

They were just little kids, Darlene and Marty both, and she knew she shouldn't expect them to act grown up. They were *good* kids and she loved them, and they didn't mean to get on her nerves; she shouldn't get irritated and hateful with them. They loved to do things that pleased her. They delighted in her praise and her approval, and when she did lose her patience with them, the hurt showed immediately in their sad eyes.

Alisa wished she could turn her mind off, just stop thinking for a little while. She felt tears slip from beneath her closed lids, and she could feel that Darlene had relaxed. Her whispery, even breathing meant that she had fallen asleep.

Carefully, gently, she turned over onto her other side and drew her little sister close. With a brief fluttering of her eyelashes and then a deep sigh, Darlene snuggled against her once more and settled back into sleep.

They had barely finished their late breakfast when the telephone rang. Alisa went to answer it.

"I didn't wake you, did I?" someone asked, and for a moment she was at a loss. Then she knew it was Paul's voice.

"Gosh, no," she said. "We've been awake for a long time. I have a little brother and sister, remember? When they get up, everybody gets up."

"Okay, then can I come over? Or . . . maybe I shouldn't. I forgot for a minute that you said your mother's sick."

"Just a second," she told him. She covered the mouthpiece and turned to her father. "Paul Heyser wants to come over," she said. "Will that be all right?"

At her father's nod, she turned back to the phone, a little surprised at the sudden lift in her spirits. "It's okay, Paul," she said. "Come on over."

Then she hurried to give her short hair a quick brushing and to apply a touch of lip gloss and cologne. For a brief moment she studied her reflection in the mirror, then turned away. She wasn't beautiful, certainly; both her face and body were too thin for that. But she knew she wasn't unattractive, either. Though she accepted dates mostly just for school activities, it was by her own choice. Boys seemed to like her well enough. Having a date for a party or dance had never been a real problem. But she'd never dated anyone quite like Paul Heyser. Although they were in the same grade, he seemed older than the other boys, more thoughtful and maybe even more difficult because of that tendency toward moodiness and his stilted efforts at conversation.

It wouldn't matter, she told herself. If he wanted to talk, fine. If he wanted to be quiet, that was all right, too. She had enough problems already, and she wasn't about to get all out of sorts about any boy!

He arrived a few minutes later, and to her surprise he was quickly at ease with her father, talking and laughing with no hesitation whatever. Of course Bernard Wilson did have an easy, accepting manner that made people feel comfortable, but still, Paul was only sixteen or seventeen. Weren't teenage boys always shy, intimidated by older men? Especially with the fathers of the girls they went to visit?

But she was pleased. Sitting across the room from Paul, she watched him and listened to his questions and comments. He even *sounded* older than he was as he talked about his father's business and recounted an incident from his previous summer's visit.

It was interesting to watch and listen, and she smiled when Paul asked her father about the stack of textbooks beside his chair. He seemed surprised but admiring when Bernard explained that he was working for a degree that would enable him to return to work in aeronautics.

Some people did not react as Paul was doing when they learned that her father wasn't "working." Some suggested by their attitude that they considered her father an irresponsible and selfish man, allowing his family to do without things while he acted like a kid, going back to school. He was aware of such feelings, too. She had overheard him discussing it with her mother, the way a few people who didn't know him well took such care to avoid the subject of his unemployment.

Alisa had found the same awkwardness in people who should have inquired about her mother, only it was much worse. While people hesitated in asking her father about his situation face to face, they showed no such reluctance in asking Alisa about him. But with her mother's illness, it was different. Everyone seemed to know about it; she could tell that by the way they talked to her. But few ever actually asked about her mother. It was easier with the few who did ask instead of pretending that nothing was wrong, for that required that she pretend as well, and she knew what was responsible for the difference. It was because of the nature of her mother's illness—because she was in a psychiatric ward.

"Alisa?"

She looked up, bewildered. She'd been woolgathering again, unaware that someone had been talking to her.

"Sorry, I was . . . daydreaming, I guess," she said. "What did you say?" She didn't even know whether it had been her father or Paul who had addressed her.

"We were talking about the project," Paul said.

"What project?"

"You really *were* out of touch," her father said, laughing. "*Your* project. Cleaning up South Rutland. Paul seems to have some good ideas; you should've been listening."

"That is, if you're interested in trying it," Paul said. "I called Mister Reed yesterday, and he liked the idea of the two of us working as partners. I mean, if you want to."

"Did you tell him about it, about what a big and probably impossible project it is?"

"No," Paul said. "He asked, but since I wasn't sure how you felt about it, I said we'd tell him on Monday. But I don't think it's so impossible, Alisa. It probably won't be easy, and maybe we could never make it work one hundred percent, but it's worth trying. I'm almost certain that it's worth trying."

His enthusiasm was hard to resist, and she found her interest aroused once more, although the fear of a crashing failure still lurked all too close to the surface of her thoughts.

"All right," she finally said. "I'll admit that I can't quite get it out of my mind and that I've got a few half-developed ideas of my own. So I guess we might as well just wade in and get our feet wet. Where should we begin?"

Chapter Twelve

AN HOUR LATER Alisa got up from her chair at the kitchen table where they had been working. "I think we've earned a break," she told Paul. "How about some lemonade? And there's half a cake left, too."

At that point Darlene wandered in. "Darlene, will you get the cake platter?" she asked. "I'm going to make lemonade for everyone."

"Can I cut it, too?" her little sister asked. "I'll be real careful; I promise."

"Okay," Alisa agreed. Then, remembering what her mother would have done, she added, "But first you have to figure out how many slices to cut and how to divide the cake evenly. Do you think you can do that?"

"I can count the slices," Darlene replied with confidence. "One for Daddy and one for me. That's two. Then one for you and one for Paul. That's two more, and two plus two makes four. Then add one for Marty, and that's five."

Then she placed the knife in the center of the half circle of cake and paused, nibbling at her lower lip and frowning in concentration. Alisa, busy mixing the lemonade, didn't notice, but Paul watched the eight-year-old curiously.

"What's the problem?" he finally asked Darlene when her quandary continued and she didn't cut the cake.

"I can't do it, I don't think," she said to him. Her disappointment was as obvious as her puzzlement had been a moment earlier. "If I cut it here, in the middle, both sides will be the same. But one side needs three slices and the other side needs only two."

"I see," Paul said. "That is a problem. Tell you what, we can just tell Alisa that she can't have a slice; then there'll only be four. That's two on each side. It would be easier that way, wouldn't it?"

"But it wouldn't be *nice*," Darlene scolded, taking his teasing as a serious suggestion. Alisa turned to listen.

"You're absolutely right, Darlene," Paul said, humble now. "I think I can help you to cut five slices, though. Shall I show you?"

But Darlene wasn't listening. Alisa noticed her little sister's chin raise in determination as a smile lit her elfin face.

"Now I know what to do," she said. "I can make *six* slices of cake. That'll be three on each side."

"But who will eat the extra slice?" Paul asked. Alisa smiled, watching and listening. Though Paul had said he hadn't been around little kids very much, he was doing all right. And she, too, wondered what Darlene had in mind.

"Mama will get the other piece," Darlene informed them with a sparkling smile. "Our mama's in the hospital, see, but we're going to visit her tomorrow, and I'm going to wrap up a piece of cake real careful and take it to her. I bet she'll *love* it. I bet they never give her any cake this good in that old hospital!"

"That's the nicest idea I've heard all day, Darlene," Paul said, leaning over to give her a little hug. Then he turned to Alisa, searching for words for his thought that would not disturb Darlene.

"In hospitals there are some pretty strict dietary restrictions," he said. "Do you think . . ."

"It'll be okay," Alisa replied. She hadn't explained the nature of her mother's illness to Paul.

"Our mama's got bad depression," Darlene said, even as she concentrated on making the first cut in the cake. "Sherry Richmond said she's crazy, but she's not. She feels real bad, but I'll bet this cake will make her feel more better. Will you help me wrap it up good, Alisa?"

"I'll bet you're exactly right, Darlene," Paul said with an easy smile that changed his whole appearance. "I know one thing: If you brought me a present like that, it would make *me* feel better, even if I was depressed."

With a grateful sigh, Alisa moved to help Darlene finish cutting the cake and wrap a slice for her mother. Then she poured lemonade and sent Darlene for her father and brother. "My mother's in a psychiatric ward," she murmured to Paul when they were alone.

"That's a little difficult," he replied simply. "My mother spent a few weeks there last summer. She developed a drinking problem after she and Dad split up. But she's well now.''

''That's great,'' Alisa said. ''I guess your mother must have a lot of willpower.''

''Oh, I don't know about that,'' Paul replied in a flat voice. ''I think all they did was convince her that booze was bad for her complexion or something. My mother worries a *lot* about her looks.''

Alisa wanted to reply, but her father and Marty came into the kitchen then, and they concentrated on the cake and lemonade.

''Well, have you two gotten anywhere yet?'' her father asked when he'd finished.

''Maybe,'' Alisa replied. ''We've listed our ideas, and we've made a rough sketch of the area we want to concentrate on. It's pretty big, though—seventeen blocks. Do you think we should cut it down some to make it easier?''

''If it'll work with one square block, it ought to work with seventeen,'' her father replied. ''Why think small? I heard something the other day that seems to fit this situation: If it was easy, someone else would have already done it!''

Laughing, Alisa handed him the sheet of paper she'd been making notes on, and he read it with interest. ''You've even made a clear statement of what you want to achieve,'' he observed, smiling up at them. ''That's very good. It's easier to get somewhere if you know just exactly where you're trying to go. Your plans look fine to me. Put up posters in South Rutland, get radio and newspaper advertisements, and visit a city council meeting to ask for support. This sounds to me like a good way to begin.''

''But we have no idea how to get those things accomplished,'' Paul said, ''except for the posters. Advertising's expensive. And we're both kind of scared about attending the city council meeting.''

''Except for the executive sessions, the meetings are open to the public,'' Mr. Wilson said. ''I don't want to predict their response, but they will listen to you. I suggest that you plan what you'll say very carefully, though. If you have a plan, they won't be able to intimidate you because you'll have confidence. About the advertising, though—it's entirely possible that you can get it free, as public-service announcements. Plan those carefully, too, before you approach the newspaper and radio people. Know just what you want, so you won't waste their time or seem like you're not serious and determined. You've got a day off from school this week, don't you, for that teachers' workshop? That'll give you a little more time to work on this.''

In English class the next day a few students had good ideas for trying to test Thoreau's—and Mr. Reed's—idea about how to make a difference in society. One girl who was known for her great love of animals was determined to achieve more efficiency and effectiveness at the city dog pound. She had already enlisted the help of a local veterinarian, and Mr. Reed heartily approved of her plan. There were others, mostly on a smaller scale of endeavor, and to some students Mr. Reed urged further thought and planning.

Then he turned to Alisa. ''Paul tells me that you

and he have a project in mind, too," he said. "Tell us about it."

So she told them, and the reaction of her classmates ranged from wholehearted enthusiasm to observations about guaranteed, one hundred percent failure.

Mr. Reed, however, was speechless, and she shrank inside herself. Did he think she had lost her mind completely? Hearing her own voice describing the plan, she had clearly seen what an enormous undertaking it was, and she fervently wished she had never agreed to tell Paul about it on the Friday before.

"It's . . . an absolutely remarkable idea," Mr. Reed finally said. "Frankly, I'm dumbfounded. I wasn't prepared for anything like this!"

Alisa stared hard at her desk top and wondered whether Paul felt as conspicuous as she did. The room grew quiet, waiting for Mr. Reed's further comments. He leaned against the front of his desk, reaching to stroke the back of his head, his face immobile.

Then he stood up straight, and a smile creased the corners of his eyes and mouth. "You know something?" he said, "It'll work! It really will work. There's surely a way to do it, to do everything you've suggested. With some planning and a lot of effort, I really believe you can succeed in giving South Rutland a whole new . . . a face-lift, so to speak. I'm very impressed with you two. But it's not going to be easy, and you'll have to muster some powerful determination."

The dismissal bell rang just then, and everyone hurried toward the door. Mr. Reed called out, "Wait a minute, you two," and Alisa put her books back on her desk and sat down. She felt a little breathless—and suddenly hollow and scared.

"What have we gotten ourselves into?" Paul whispered from behind her. "I guess I just didn't realize how . . . do you realize that he actually thinks we can *do* this?"

Alisa nodded and swallowed. "We can't back down now, can we?" she whispered back. "We're in it up to our necks."

Then the room was empty except for the three of them, and Mr. Reed sat down heavily. Only then could they see that he was tired.

"You've dreamed up a real giant-sized project," he said to them. "I'm proud of you for thinking of it, of such a worthwhile thing to try. If it succeeds, the whole town will benefit, but especially those who live on the south side. Have you given much thought to how you'll approach it?"

"We'll make posters," Paul said. "I can draw a little bit. But we haven't even figured out where we'll get the poster board and paint and stuff."

"I can help you there," Mr. Reed said. "In a minute I'll go and get you what you'll need from the supply room. Since it's sort of a school project, it's legitimate. How about the rest—the advertising, for instance?"

"We really don't know how to do that," Alisa admitted. "We thought we'd just go to the newspaper office and the radio station and tell them what we're doing and ask if they'll help. Dad said they might consider it a community-service thing and do it free."

Mr. Reed nodded thoughtfully. "The thing to do when you're unsure how to proceed is to get an expert's advice," he mused. "You'll need to comprehend an awful lot about human behavior in a short time. Let's go and talk to Mrs. Birnam; with her background in psychology, she's sure to be able to help." He started to rise, but Alisa remembered that her father was picking her up.

"I can't today," she said. "My Dad's waiting for me. We have a lot to do this evening." She felt bad about it, with Mr. Reed so willing to help.

"That's probably better, anyway," he said. "I'll mention it to Mrs. Birnam myself and see if she can talk with you two for a few minutes after school tomorrow. Can you do that? It'll give her a little time to think it over."

They agreed, and Mr. Reed said, "Go on and meet your father, Alisa. And you come with me, Paul. We'll raid the supply room."

She was halfway out of the room when he called to her. "I've been forgetting to ask, Alisa. Is your mother getting any better yet?"

"The doctor thinks so," she replied comfortably. "We're going to visit for the first time this evening."

"That's a good indication that she's improving, then," he said. "I also wondered about something else, not exactly on the same level of importance. How'd the broiled fish come out?"

80

She smiled, mostly at the puzzled expression on Paul's face. "It was great, Mister Reed," she said, and left them.

Chapter Thirteen

"You're late," her father observed when she got into his car in front of the school. "What took you so long? We've got a lot to do." It wasn't like him to grumble, and for a moment she was taken aback.

Then she thought perhaps she could see what was wrong, the same thing that had lingered in her thoughts all day long. They were going for their first visit to the hospital. He hadn't seen his wife for almost a week, and he was both eager to see her and anxious about her condition.

"I'm sorry, Dad," she said. "Mister Reed kept Paul and me for a few minutes. He was excited about our project, and he had a couple of things to say. But I told him I had to leave."

"It's all right, Alisa," her father said. "I'm a little bit on edge. But Doctor Marshall's meeting us at six o'clock, and he wants us to see him first. So I can't hurry things along, anyway."

"We're supposed to stop by the nursery for Mrs. Carter," she reminded him. "Then it'll take a little while to get Darlene and Marty ready. We'll have plenty of time, only we'll have to eat a sandwich before we go instead of fixing a regular meal.''

''I thought about that,'' he said. ''Maybe we can stop somewhere on our way back home. But don't mention it to the kids. We might not want to do that, after all.''

She nodded. ''We can always come back home and fix a hamburger if we need to,'' she said.

They were in front of the nursery then, and Alisa got out. There were a few azalea bushes in front of the building, as Mrs. Carter had said. They were awfully pretty, but she opened the door and went inside. She'd never been in the nursery before, and the mass of color dazed her. Pot after pot of begonias filled the shelves along one wall and hung in pots from wires above, in every imaginable shade from white to blazing red. Another shelf exploded with even more brilliance and variety. They were little plants in pots not as big as her fist, but the leaves were a dozen different tones of green, and there were blossoms of all shapes and sizes. The only ones she could identify on that shelf were the marigolds.

''May I help you with something?''

The voice startled her; she'd been so enchanted with the flowers that she hadn't seen the short, chubby man approaching. He was shiny bald on top, but around the sides and back of his head a regular hedge of a curious mix of red and gray hair grew almost like a crown that had slipped a little. His face was the liveliest she had ever seen. He wore a smile from ear to ear, and somehow she knew that his smile was both typical and genuine.

"I came to look at azalea bushes," she said, "but everything's so bright and beautiful, it's practically taken my breath away!"

"Isn't it the truth, though!" he agreed, beaming. "Young lady, my name is Arthur McLeary, and I happen to think I'm the luckiest man in the world. And who would you be?"

"Why . . . I'm Alisa Wilson," she said. Then she couldn't resist. His remark, she felt certain, had been intentional; she was expected to respond. "Why are you the luckiest man in the world?" she asked.

Impossible as it seemed, his smile grew; he radiated cheer and hope. "Because I spend my days here, where there's so much color and freshness and *life*. There are a hundred different smells, too, right down to the rich dirt in these flowerpots, and all of them are fine," he said. "Now, tell the truth; except for the other kind of nursery, where the newborn babies are sleeping and squalling and kicking their little legs in the air and raising Cain, have you ever seen a place any more filled with *life*?"

Dazed by his vitality and enthusiasm, she could only smile and agree with him.

"But you wanted the azaleas," he remembered. "Follow me, ma'am. Have I ever got azaleas for you!"

She followed him through another door, and they were in an immense glass-roofed room, glorious with dazzling color and scent. He led her to the azaleas on the far side of the room, where she stood, awed by the stunning array. There were soft reds and blazing fire-reds, pink, lavender, and the purest white she'd ever seen. She could only stand and stare, it was all so breathtaking.

But her father awaited. "I . . . I want the lavender, two of them," she finally said. "They're for a neighbor, and she likes lavender best. But how much are they? She said she can't afford much."

"Well, now, there's a price for everyone," Mr. McLeary said, looking about him and then pointing. "Those are twelve dollars each. Over here we have some not quite so big for seven, and these in this area are five. Over there I have some smaller ones. They're three-fifty each. Just choose the size you want and then pick out as many as you need."

Moments later Alisa had selected two of the five-dollar pots. Mr. McLeary carried them to the front room, where she paid with her own money. Surely Mrs. Carter would be pleased and willing to take them, but if she didn't, Alisa decided, the bushes would look wonderful at either end of the Wilsons' front porch.

Back in the car with her father, Alisa leaned over the lovely, delicate lavender blossoms to inhale the heady fragrance. And she couldn't stop smiling.

"Dad, you've just got to go inside Mister McLeary's nursery sometime soon," she said. "It's so great, with all the flowers. And he's just the neatest man I've ever seen."

"Arthur McLeary, isn't it?" her father asked, and she nodded. "I remember him," he went on. "He was full of life; he seemed to be moving even when he was sitting still, we used to say in high school. We also used to say that Art must've kissed the Blarney stone, since he was never short of something to say. He was always invited to every party back then, too. One thing we could count on: If Arthur was anywhere near, there wasn't a chance that things would get dull or tiresome.''

"Was he always so positive?'' Alisa wondered. "You know, it's kind of odd. I wondered how old he was, but there was just no way to even guess.''

Chuckling, her father agreed. "Art's a couple of years older than I am, best I recall,'' he said. "Your mother dropped in there about a month ago, before she . . . stopped getting out anywhere. And she mentioned the same thing. She said he was ageless.''

They rode in silence until they reached Mrs. Carter's house. Quickly Alisa got out, lifting the flowerpots, and started up the walk.

"Oh, my!'' Mrs. Carter cried before she'd even reached the porch. "Oh, my goodness! They're just the prettiest things I've ever seen in my whole life!''

The woman's heavy, unhappy face was transformed before Alisa's eyes as Mrs. Carter reached as if to touch the plants, then drew her hand back and merely sat there as if drinking them in.

"If I'd a'known they'd be this pretty up close,'' she murmured, "I woulda already had some of these.''

She paid Alisa gladly, even offering her money for getting the flowers for her. Alisa, enjoying Mrs. Carter's pleasure, refused the extra money.

"If you like, I'll stop by tomorrow and help you set them in your yard,'' she said. "I have to go now, though. Shall I stop by tomorrow?''

"That would be mighty nice,'' Mrs. Carter replied softly, smiling. "Your help will be welcome. And I just can't tell you how much I appreciate your doin' this for me."

Her father had heard the conversation, and when Alisa came back to the car, he said, "Looks like Meredith was right about Mrs. Carter, wouldn't you say? She didn't seem much like her regular complaining, despairing self."

Darlene and Marty were already on the front porch, waiting for them. She had taken more time than she'd intended.

"Come on, kids," she said. "Let's get cleaned up and get a sandwich. It'll be time for us to leave soon."

"We *hurried*," Marty said. "Why can't we just go right now? I'm not hungry, anyway!"

"Sorry, son," his father replied, ruffling his hair. "You'll have to wash up and change your clothes first, like your sister said. But don't worry; we'll get there in plenty of time."

Unexpectedly overcome with a fit of nervousness, Alisa couldn't seem to do anything right. She dropped a slice of ham on the floor while she fixed the sandwiches, and tears blurred her vision until she wiped her eyes. Then, when the sandwiches were ready at last and she took her turn in the bathroom, she couldn't find the toothpaste. Just as she was about to yell at her sister and brother, there it was, right before her eyes.

A button fell off her blouse while she was dressing, and then the needle simply would not be threaded. She threw the blouse to the floor and began looking for another, but everything looked ugly all at once, and she barely kept herself from crying about that.

It didn't make any sense! What was wrong with her? It had been on her mind all day long, through everything else that had happened, and she'd been excited, like Marty. She wanted very much to see her mother. So why was she fumbling and messing up and fighting to hold back her tears?

Chapter Fourteen

HER EMOTIONS IN turmoil, Alisa paid little attention to Marty and Darlene's chatter in the backseat, nor was she much aware of her father's presence until she realized that he had said something.

She looked toward him, but he hadn't been talking to her. "Incompetent drivers!" he muttered as someone passed, startling him. A scowl tightened his typically pleasant features, and he took one hand from the steering wheel to adjust the rearview mirror. By the time he was satisfied with the position of the mirror, Alisa felt certain that it was in the exact place it had been at the start.

"Scoot *over*," she heard then from the backseat. "You're gonna squash Mama's cake!"

"I can't scoot over!" Marty retorted.

"You're just being a big pain," Darlene accused. Then: "Alisa, make him scoot over. He's almost sitting on the cake I'm bringing to Mama." The whining note underlying her words grated on Alisa's nerves, and she turned to look.

"Darlene, you can see there's no room," she said sharply. "You move closer to the window instead. And why must the cake lie in the seat? Hold it in your lap!''

''But I'm afraid *I'll* squash it,'' her little sister replied.

''Then give it to me.''

''No, *I'm* bringing it,'' Darlene protested. ''It was my idea.''

''Darlene, hand me the cake this minute,'' Alisa said. ''I'll give it back to you when we get there!''

Reluctant, moving with deliberately exaggerated slowness, Darlene handed the tinfoil-wrapped slice of cake forward. Very much aware of the throbbing tension that pulled at the back of her neck, Alisa took the package and turned around to face forward once again.

''See there, I *told* you I didn't have any more room,'' Marty chortled, and before Darlene could respond, their father said, ''That's enough, do you hear? Not another word of quarreling while we're in the car!''

We're some warm and loving family, Alisa thought darkly. It's stupid; we haven't seen Mom for nearly a week, and instead of being glad and eager, we're acting like it's something to dread.

But wasn't it, in a way? Probably it lurked somewhere near the surface in the consciousness of all four of them, the fear that she would be the same: dull, lifeless, unresponsive, uninterested. It was like seeing a stranger who looked a bit like Meredith Wilson and wore her clothes but possessed none of her vitality and joy.

The silence in the car grew and multiplied and expanded until the air all but suffocated her, and she moved the little handle marked "vent" until she could feel the rush of cool air on her ankles. It helped a bit, and the sound also muffled what she thought was probably a sniffling noise from behind her.

This could not go on. Another minute and *she'd* be crying!

"Listen, everyone," Alisa said in a firm, controlled voice that concealed her tremulous nerves, "we're going to see Mom, for goodness sake! What're we so grouchy for? After just a couple of days of the new treatment, Doctor Marshall told us that she was already improving. And it's been a few days more now. She's getting well faster this time, and we've got to show how glad we are instead of picking at one another."

Her father cleared his throat. "Alisa's right," he said. "We mustn't go up there with long faces. That would worry your mother instead of helping her. We're almost there now, so get out your smiles and dust 'em off, smooth 'em out, and put 'em on."

They heard Marty's giggle then. Darlene didn't respond, but at least there were no more sniffles.

Then, after a moment's silence, she heard a timid, unsure question, but the whining note had disappeared. "Alisa, do you think Mama will really like my present?"

"Of course she'll like it," Alisa replied, praying that her mother would be well enough to recognize the tremendous importance of a clumsily wrapped, not very good two-day-old slice of cake.

"Remember when you used to bring Mom a handful of dandelions with the stems all broken off?'' she asked Darlene. ''Mom put water in a red bowl and put the flowers in, and they floated. Remember?''

''I 'member that!'' Darlene cried. ''They were so pretty!''

''Right,'' Alisa said, ''and she'll like your gift today, too. But listen . . . try not to be too disappointed if Mom doesn't . . . talk very much. Just remember that the doctor said she's getting better.''

''I've got a secret to tell Mama,'' Marty announced then. ''She's really gonna like it, and nobody knows it yet, 'cept me. That's my present.''

Poor kid, Alisa thought, I should have made sure he had a present for Mom, too, so he wouldn't feel left out. Why didn't I think of that?

''Just being together for a little while is going to be a fine present, kids,'' their father said as he turned off the busy street into the immense parking lot at St. Luke's Hospital.

The elevator seemed to take forever. Marty fidgeted while Darlene cradled her gift as if it were eggs. Their father stared at his feet, and Alisa stared at the rows of buttons on the elevator wall. Then suddenly they felt an uncomfortable lurch, and the doors slid noiselessly open.

Dr. Marshall waited at a desk near the elevator, right out in the hall. He came to shake their father's hand, smiling.

''So you're here, and right on time,'' he observed. ''I'm glad to see you again. But this conference, I'm happy to tell you, isn't nearly so necessary as I had first believed.''

"Do you mean. . . ?" Bernard Wilson couldn't finish the question, but Dr. Marshall nodded, still smiling, and his gray eyes were kind and gentle.

"Your wife is responding marvelously to the new medicine," he said. "You see, Mister Wilson, we still do not really understand what causes severe depression. Or rather, we know of many causes, or contributing factors. The difficulty lies in discovering the right treatment. A medicine may work miracles for one patient yet have no effect at all on another."

"So . . . do you feel that this improvement isn't just a temporary thing, that it might be an honest-to-God cure?"

"Mister Wilson, we're still quite reluctant to use the word 'cure' when we're dealing with this kind of condition. But still . . . well, go on and see her. I think you'll see what I mean. She's in the visitors' lounge just around the corner."

They started ahead, eager and expectant, but Dr. Marshall spoke once more, and they paused.

"There's just one thing," he said, not so enthusiastically. "You may feel that Meredith should go home right away, but you must not rush things. It's especially critical that she remain here awhile longer so that we can monitor everything. *Especially* critical. We can't risk losing a single inch of ground we've gained. Will you try to remember that?"

They were so silent, it seemed to Alisa that nobody even breathed as they approached the door to the visitors' lounge. Then they were there, and they saw her.

She sat in a familiar pose with her legs drawn

up, her feet half-tucked under her in the chair, reading a magazine. In the light from the reading lamp her silky dark brown hair framed her face in delicate waves, and she wore makeup, as she'd always done when she was well. Slender and lovely, she was wearing the pretty floral print dress that Alisa had packed along with nightgowns and toilet articles on that night when it had seemed as if her mother would never again take an interest in her appearance.

Alisa felt tears stinging her eyes. She had never before realized with such joy that her mother was so very beautiful.

"Mama!" Marty and Darlene cried at once, rushing to her and throwing their arms around her. Their mother dropped the magazine and straightened in the chair, drawing them to her fiercely, her marvelous eyes brimming.

Then somehow Alisa was within the circle of her mother's loving embrace as well, and the overwhelming feeling of peace and safety nearly took her breath away.

After the first rush of greeting, they moved to a comfortable sofa where their father could sit beside her, too. In their excitement at the miraculous extent of Meredith's recovery, the words tumbled over one another when they all tried to talk at once.

"Doctor Marshall's almost as thrilled as I am," she told them. "He tells me that it's practically unheard of for the medicine to have this effect in less than two weeks at the very least. But I am *so* much better. I can hardly wait for him to say I can come home."

They talked of everything, and her mother praised the cake, which must have been a little stale, and ate every bite. Then, as though he'd been waiting for just the right moment, Marty told her his secret.

"My teacher helped me grow a plant," he said, unaware of his mother's puzzled glance of inquiry at her husband, "and it's already come up out of the dirt, and it has two little green leaves on it, and pretty soon now I can bring it home and put it in the backyard, and it's gonna be just for you. And guess what, Mama: It's a happiness plant!"

"That's wonderful, Marty," his mother said, hugging him while he smiled from ear to ear. "Imagine that—a happiness plant. How can I ever wait to see it?"

"But what's your secret, Marty?" Darlene asked. "You already told us about your plant last week. That was no secret."

"But I didn't tell you that it was for Mama and that it was already *growing* and had leaves and everything," Marty said. "I saved that part since Friday, and I didn't tell anybody."

"It's a fine secret, Marty," his mother said. "Now tell me, kids, has your father been behaving himself and doing his homework?"

They talked for a while then about her father's classes, his grades, and how soon he would be ready to graduate. It was a cheerful talk, for he would finish his course work in just a few more weeks. Then he would only have one major research paper to write.

It was beginning to look as if they might make

it, after all! Her mother was so much improved that it was almost beyond comprehension, with only a suggestion of tiredness still evident. And her father was making so much progress, too. It was almost too exciting to bear, and there was absolutely no reason for the tears that threatened to burst forth at any moment.

Chapter Fifteen

PAUL HAD SAID that he could draw a little bit, but Alisa gasped in surprise when he showed her what he had done the evening before. He had taken the poster board home with him and had lightly sketched pictures and lettering on four sheets.

Two were delightful cartoons, and the other two were simple but effective demonstrations. One depicted a man, woman, and child and even their dog picking up trash. The dog stood on his hind legs, dropping a Styrofoam tray into a trash can sporting the lettering "South Rutland, a community with pride." Another showed before and after pictures of a plain frame house. In the "before" drawing, the screens were torn, the porch had a couple of boards missing, and the yard was littered. The "after" picture was the same house with the repairs made and a few simple plants replacing the litter. Under the drawings were the plain block letters "South Rutland." Alisa felt that the poster spoke volumes, especially because the changes were so simple and inexpensive yet made an astounding difference.

She was clearly delighted with his work, and he

in turn seemed deeply pleased by her reaction. They colored the four posters with bright marking pens during study hall and took them to show to Mr. Reed between classes.

"These seem exactly right to me," he said. "You've managed to make community improvement desirable without giving offense, and you've shown how much easy, inexpensive improvements can help. Frankly, I'm rather surprised, Paul. Your drawing indicates an awfully mature understanding."

"Thanks," Paul said, blushing, "but to tell the truth, it wasn't all my doing. In my first try at the before and after pictures, I had the house practically remodeled. Then my mother asked what I was doing. When I explained, she said I'd gone too far. She said I was making it look too impossible and suggested that I ought to tone it down some. Then I saw that she was right. Now and then my mother surprises me."

Mr. Reed nodded. "You've done well," he said, "but you'll need a lot more of these, I think. And don't forget, Mrs. Birnam will be here for a few minutes after school. I think she'll have some very useful information to make your project go more smoothly."

Mrs. Birnam taught general psychology, and both Paul and Alisa were in her fifth-hour class. Neither of them had said anything about Mr. Reed's suggestion that she advise them, but Alisa wondered how she could be of help. She was certainly nice enough, and her class had been interesting. She was even pretty, a tall, blue-eyed blond woman about Mr. Reed's age. But the things they had studied so far didn't seem to have any direct application to their project.

After English class, in which they had taken an essay test on Thoreau's "Civil Disobedience," she came into the room and began talking. She didn't waste any time.

"Mister Reed has told me about the project you two are attempting," she said, "and I find it an utterly intriguing idea. Since yesterday I've given it a lot of thought, and it occurs to me that I won't be telling you anything that you don't already know. Still, it might help for you to be reminded of a few concepts so you can consciously apply them to your project.

"There are two basic ways to influence people to change their behavior. One is by force, which is never completely successful because we naturally resent that kind of pressure, and we rebel. You'll be familiar with one aspect of this method, which is the subtle force we exert by making people feel guilty about something; they will usually do what we want under that kind of pressure in an attempt to relieve the guilt feelings. Parents and children use this method on each other all the time. It often works, but the result isn't very satisfactory, probably because the motivation is wrong.

"The second method is far more preferable. We'll call it inspiration. Give someone a reason to *want* to change his behavior. But always keep this in mind: You must not try to make the changes yourself. You may make subtle suggestions, and you may be helpful and supportive and encouraging, but unless people are able to feel that they have *chosen* to change and have done the necessary work themselves, been in *control* of the changes, they will not do anything. Even without consciously thinking about it, they will know that there is no satisfaction, no pleasure in an accomplishment if someone else made the decisions and did the work.

"The two of you will need to think this over very carefully and devise a way to use this principle at every step. I won't make any suggestions myself today, but after you think it over, feel free to consult me if you need to. I would love to be involved if you need me."

Glancing at Paul, Alisa could almost see the wheels turning. She, too, was impressed, but that was a bit odd. Mrs. Birnam *hadn't* told them anything really new, but to deliberately apply principles of human behavior was an exciting prospect. Already she was anxious to find some quiet time and go to work—inside her own mind.

After a moment Mrs. Birnam began again. "The other concept that you'll need to stay attentive to is the need of all of us to *belong*, to be a part of a group. Now, what I'm going to say may seem discriminatory at first, but if you'll allow yourselves to be objective, I believe you will understand and agree with me.

"Humans are social beings. We must participate, have some kind of interaction with others. The poet John Donne said, 'No man is an island,' and he was precisely correct. Now, I happen to believe that you have an excellent chance of success in this project simply because it *is* a low-income area."

Neither Alisa nor Paul responded, but she had certainly gotten their attention. Even Mr. Reed watched her with lifted brows.

"People who live on small, often inadequate incomes simply cannot afford many of the social activities that are common to more well-to-do folk," Mrs. Birnam said. "You'll find that membership in nearly all dues-paying organizations is made up of economically middle- and upper-class people. Same thing with sports groups, even cultural or craft-oriented clubs like little theaters and garden clubs. There's always some expense involved, not to mention the need for baby-sitters, transportation, and 'proper' attire.

"This doesn't mean that low-income families have no opportunity for socializing, but whether you like the sound of it or not, the fact is that their opportunities are limited. They have fewer chances to be publicly recognized, to be designated as officers, as leaders, as people who *do* things.

"Now listen: *All* people like to do good things, to have a chance to feel good about themselves. Even if someone should say that he doesn't want to do good things, you can count on this: His saying that is a defense because he feels inadequate in ability, funding, or opportunity.

"Now I'll sum it up. Inspire the people in South Rutland to *want* to improve the appearance of the community. Be optimistic, encouraging, and helpful but allow *them* to figure out how to do it and to be recognized publicly for their achievements. Find a way to designate some as leaders. And finally, keep this in mind: If you can get some financial backing, fine. But poor people don't need to be reminded that they're poor. Believe me, they know it all the time. I speak from experience.''

Such concentrated, intense instruction was the last thing Alisa had expected, and she left the classroom in a daze. Her thoughts whirled; she didn't want to forget a word of Mrs. Birnam's lecture. Paul walked beside her, but neither spoke until they were outside.

''Wow,'' Paul said in a near whisper, ''she really socked it to us, didn't she?''

Alisa nodded. ''It was . . . stupendous. Amazing. And yet no particular part of it was all that unique. I wonder why . . .''

''Saying it all *together* like that. In a package, almost,'' Paul said, answering her uncompleted question. ''It's like . . . we can *use* what she said. By the way, did we thank her?''

''I think so,'' Alisa replied, laughing. ''I'm not sure, though. We can do it tomorrow. And speaking of tomorrow, I have to go. See you in the morning.''

''Okay if I drive you home?'' Paul asked.

''Sure. Yes, that'll help. But not home; I have to stop at Mrs. Carter's house first.''

By the time they reached Mrs. Carter's, Alisa had explained about the azalea bushes.

''Do you think she'll mind if I help?'' Paul asked.

''Probably not,'' Alisa replied. ''*I* won't mind. I'm not all that skilled at using a shovel.''

Mrs. Carter was pleased to see both of them. She made her way off the porch to supervise the planting, and Alisa saw that the woman really did walk with difficulty. A wave of guilt washed over her; she had called the woman lazy so many times, but thankfully, only in her own thoughts.

Mrs. Carter showed Paul where she wanted the flowers and told him where to find the shovel. Then, while he worked, she asked Alisa about her mother. So many times before, Alisa had resented Mrs. Carter's questioning, calling it nosiness and worse. But the resentment, the awkwardness and reluctance to discuss it, all seemed to have disappeared.

"Mom's much better," she said. "She was cheerful and lively, and we had a fine visit. They're using a new medicine this time, something about some necessary chemical or mineral that she didn't have enough of. I don't understand it really, but the new treatment is working wonders. Doctor Marshall didn't exactly say so, but Dad and I both have the impression that she'll only have to stay in the hospital about two more weeks."

"That's fine; that's mighty nice to hear," Mrs. Carter said with sincere pleasure. "Do you reckon maybe they've found a real cure this time?"

"Maybe," Alisa said. "We hope so. In fact, we really think so. But Doctor Marshall won't go quite that far yet. We'll just have to wait and see."

Nodding, Mrs. Carter watched Paul carefully as he prepared to take the plant from the plastic pot.

"Be right careful there," she said, and he glanced up and smiled. "Now, break up that ball of roots with your hands. That's right, but handle 'em real gentle; just loosen 'em up some."

He did everything just as she instructed, and soon

one of the bushes looked as though it had been growing beside her walk all along. There were still a lot of the delicate lavender buds that hadn't yet opened. It would remain in breathtaking bloom for quite a while longer.

"Are you still thinkin' about gettin' South Rutland cleaned up some?" Mrs. Carter asked while Paul started digging the second hole.

"Well . . ." Alisa hesitated. There'd been no time to even think about Mrs. Birnam's advice, but maybe she could handle it right. "It really would make everyone feel more hopeful, don't you think?" she said. "There are lots of things that could be done to make the neighborhood so much nicer, and most of it wouldn't cost much, mostly just some work. If there was just some way to get the people together . . ."

Mrs. Carter nodded, rubbing her ample chin thoughtfully. "I've been thinkin' about it some," she said slowly. "I figured a person who don't get out much, like me, could maybe call folks up on the phone and kinda mention it. Might get a few folks interested."

"That's a wonderful idea!" Alisa cried, and at that Paul stopped to listen. "Why, I'll bet you know practically everyone on this side of town already! You said once that you've lived here for years."

"I know a lot of 'em," the woman said. "There's some new folks. They come and go, especially in some of the rent houses. But say, I reckon I could try and get everybody on this block to talkin', and some of them might talk to folks they know on the next block."

"Hey, that's great," Paul said. "We could ask for volunteers and designate someone on each block as supervisor. Mrs. Carter, you're a wonder! You'd be a perfect supervisor for your block."

The woman's smile softened and warmed her features; she beamed. "Well, now, maybe I could, at that," she said, clearly very pleased at the idea. "It'd give me something to do with my time b'sides thinking about my arthritis and wishin' I could get around like I used to do!"

Chapter Sixteen

MORE OPTIMISTIC THAN she had felt in ages, Alisa could barely contain her excitement as Paul drove her the rest of the way home and came inside with her. They hadn't planned it, but they were too excited to part just yet.

"What are you two grinning about?" her father asked as soon as he saw them. "You look as pleased as a couple of cats with a bowl of cream."

"We *did* it, Dad," Alisa cried, hugging him. "We actually *did* something—or got something started at least."

When they told him about their afternoon, he was pleased as well. "You've done fine," he said. "Now you'll have to follow through, but as Mrs. Birnam said, you must let the people take over soon."

"You don't think we should stop *now*, do you?" Paul asked. They could hear a hint of disappointment in his voice.

"Heavens, no! You can't stop. That isn't what I meant at all," Mr. Wilson said, laughing. "There'll be more for you to do than you'll want, probably. I only meant that if—*when* this thing gets rolling, you two will need to stay in the background, so to speak. But for now you'll have to make the posters and put them up on every block, and arrange to go to the city council meeting this Thursday night, and all sorts of things. Fortunately, you've got all day tomorrow to work on it.''

"All day tomorrow?'' Alisa asked, puzzled. Then she and Paul burst out laughing in the same instant.

"We forgot about it,'' Alisa said at last. "I can't believe it. We actually forgot about having tomorrow off!''

"They've been announcing the teachers' workshop on the radio for a week,'' her father said dryly. "No doubt they've mentioned it at school. Marty and Darlene certainly didn't forget. They're out in the backyard already; said they'd do their homework tomorrow night.''

"We've been so awfully busy,'' Alisa said, "and of course we knew about the workshop, but . . .''

"It's perfect, though, isn't it?'' Paul said. "I'll sketch some more posters tonight. We'll get together and finish them in the morning and put them up. And I suppose we'd better decide just what we want to say at the city council meeting, too. Do you think we ought to call someone and sort of get ourselves invited?''

"It would be the courteous thing to do,'' Alisa said, "and I'd really like to do all that tomorrow, but . . . Dad has to go to class, and Marty and Darlene will be home. And I really should try to fix a couple of decent meals, too.''

"You and Paul can finish the posters here in the

morning while I'm gone," her father said. "And if you're worried about our diet, fix a good meal this evening. We'll have cold cuts tomorrow for lunch, and I'll be here with the kids afterward. I can even make a pot of stew for supper. What you're doing is important, and a day off from school is too good a chance to miss."

They'd had fried chicken and vegetables for supper, and Darlene had helped Alisa clean up the kitchen. The cleaning woman had done a thorough job the day before, and there was little else to be done. After a pleasant, relaxing evening, they had gone to bed. Alisa could hear Darlene's rhythmic breathing in the bed across the room from hers. Her little sister was sound asleep, but Alisa lay there wide awake.

Things were certainly looking better. Everything was better, and she felt deeply grateful. She should be completely happy, Alisa told herself, and she was . . . almost. She'd been doing a pretty good job. Surely she could keep going for a couple more weeks until her mother came home. Already she felt sure that her mother wouldn't be feeling dull and sluggish from the medicine this time. She would be eager to get back to her regular activities.

In a peculiar way that almost seemed a part of her discomfort—not that her mother felt so good; that was truly wonderful. But the differences . . .

The first time her mother was ill, the whole family had existed in a kind of numb vacuum for the whole six weeks. Alisa and her father's energy had been directed toward trying to comfort and reassure

Marty and Darlene, prepare meals, and get the laundry done. With the continuous worry about her mother, that was about all they had done, and she'd experienced very little discomfort from or worry about anything outside her own family.

By the second time things had changed. While they'd been better prepared to cope at home, Alisa had become all too sensitive to the awkwardness too many people seemed to feel about her mother's being confined in a psychiatric ward. Everyone had quickly learned about it that time, probably because of the sheriff's presence. She had felt no embarrassment about it at first, since her father certainly didn't show any such feelings. But her father couldn't be with her all the time. There were neighbors to respond to and kids at school, and even a couple of teachers had seemed terribly uncomfortable when anything remotely relating to the subject of mental illness came up.

And she had begun to feel embarrassed. In spite of her certain knowledge that there was no reason, no excuse for shame, those feelings had crept into her consciousness. The more she had tried to erase the disturbing thoughts, the more they seemed to grow and occupy her mind.

This time she was older. She was supposed to be more grown up, more mature, better able to handle things. And she was. She'd been doing well, hadn't she? Her mother was being cured this time, and she would be home before much longer. Surely they would even go back to the city in a few months. If her father continued to progress so fast, he'd be able to go back to the plant, and he would certainly want to. His job was guaranteed as soon as he had that diploma. Then all the disturbing guilt would be behind her, wouldn't it? Surely she would be able to leave it all behind.

Wouldn't she?

Paul arrived early on Wednesday morning with fourteen more posters sketched and a pocketful of marking pens. Marty and Darlene wanted to help them color the posters, but Alisa said, "These are really important, kids. They have to be done very neatly, and—"

"—and you two should be able to help," Paul interposed. He placed a poster on the kitchen table for each of them and gave them pens to color with. Then he made little marks here and there on broad areas. "Just color the marked places," he said, "and Alisa and I will fill in the outside lines where it has to be so carefully done. Can you do that? It'll be a big help."

They went to work eagerly while Alisa, open-mouthed, watched them being very careful not to go beyond Paul's directions.

"For someone with no experience with little kids, you sure know how to handle things," she said. "Where've you been all this time? I could have used you in at least a million different emergencies!"

Pleased, Paul grinned as he sat to work. "It's actually kind of neat," he said. "They aren't critical. They seem to like whatever I do, and they're interested in everything, not too wrapped up with their own whims and concerns to pay attention. I guess I sound like a whiny brat, don't I? The poor rich kid who never got any personal attention?"

"It's all right, Paul," Alisa said quietly. "We all have our sensitive spots. I'm glad you like being here with us; it helps me keep a better balance, too."

"It must be really tough for you," Paul said, "but you never show it. I can't figure out how you do it, never complaining, never even acting like it's difficult for you."

"My problems are all in my own head," she said lightly. "Taking care of the kids and the house and stuff—all that's easy enough compared to what goes on in my mind." She looked up and smiled then, deliberately trying to erase what she had thoughtlessly said from Paul's mind. But he wasn't fooled.

"Seems to me," he said softly, "that if a person really was worrying about something she couldn't fix, Mrs. Birnam might be able to help."

Feeling extremely uncomfortable, as if a cold hand had reached right inside her heart, Alisa simply nodded and tried to concentrate on coloring the poster.

Tacking posters all over seventeen square blocks took a lot longer than they had anticipated. When there were only two left, a woman in slippers and a faded cotton print dress came out to meet them.

"Are you the two kids Amy Carter's talking about," she asked them, "the ones who're wanting folks to clean up the neighborhood?" Her face was grim.

A bit nervous, Alisa nodded.

"Well, I sure am glad about what you're doing," the woman said, smiling at last. "My name's Brenda Huggins, and I'm going to volunteer for block supervisor. Mrs. Carter's been calling everybody and got us all talking about it. We've about decided to have a meeting—there's plenty of people wanting to be block supervisors—in the Baptist church basement on Fourth Street Friday night. Would that be all right?"

"Well, sure," Alisa said. "That sounds great to me. Go right ahead."

"No, that's not what I meant," Mrs. Huggins said. "I meant, Would you two kids be able to be there on Friday night? Say, about six. We wouldn't want to do anything unless you-all were there. But we'd kinda like to . . . well, make some plans or something. You know, see if we can't get something done."

"Gosh, I guess we could be there. Couldn't we, Alisa?" Paul said. She could see that he was barely able to restrain his jubilation.

"I suppose so," Alisa said. "I think it'll be all right."

"You might be interested to know that Alisa and I are planning to talk to the city council members tomorrow night, too," Paul said. "They might be able to give us some support or contribute in some way."

"Well, now, how about that!" the woman said. "You two kids are really serious about all this for certain. Folks'll be glad to hear it. Does Amy Carter know about that? I'll call and tell her. It'll maybe help get more folks interested."

Without even waiting for a response, the woman turned and went toward her front door.

Paul was practically quivering with excitement. "Did you hear that?" he said. "Alisa, it's working. It's just . . . I can't believe it! They've already spread the word and even arranged a meeting to make plans. It's really wild, isn't it? Did you ever dream it would happen this fast?"

It was almost too fast, Alisa thought later when she was alone. The city council meeting on Thursday night, the block supervisor's meeting on Friday—and she'd have to be at both of them, it seemed.

What had she gotten herself into? She wasn't smart enough, and she wasn't strong enough. And if the whole thing collapsed, if the people lost interest or decided it wasn't worth the work and trouble . . .

Besides, she still had her family to take care of, didn't she? It was moving so fast, and the responsibility seemed to be mushrooming too quickly for her to handle it.

Chapter Seventeen

To HER DISMAY, Alisa found that her hands were trembling as she dressed for the city council meeting. Paul had said that the mayor, Gerald Bradshaw, had been somewhat wary even as he'd said they would be welcome. Perhaps that accounted for her nervousness—feeling that the city council members, all men, weren't exactly eager for her and Paul to attend their meeting.

Mr. Bradshaw had also asked the purpose of their attendance, but Paul had sidestepped the question with a general comment about doing something for South Rutland. They had wanted to talk with Mr. Reed about it, but he'd been called to a teachers' conference just a moment before the dismissal bell. Paul hadn't seemed particularly disturbed about going to the meeting when he'd driven Alisa home from school, and for his sake she supposed she ought to be glad. At least *one* of them wouldn't be a bundle of nerves.

It might help, she thought, if she only knew some of the men they would be facing in a little while, but she didn't. Aside from Mayor Bradshaw, she didn't even know their names. She'd never had any occasion to be especially interested in the workings of city government; there had been plenty of other things to occupy her thoughts and her time.

"You look fine, Alisa," her father said when she came out of her room at last. "That outfit is exactly right—makes you look like a young lady. In case you don't know the difference, that's a shade more mature than just being a teenager."

He was trying, with his teasing compliments, to put her at ease. She was grateful for his effort, but as far as she could tell, it wasn't helping very much. For what must have been the hundredth time that day, she wished . . . well, not that she'd never gotten involved, exactly, but at least that she'd had more time to get into the right frame of mind for what lay ahead.

"I'm shaking inside, Dad," she said. "Would you mind trying just a little harder to encourage me?"

He laughed and then sobered. "I'll do exactly that," he said, looking her right in the eye. "The men you'll see tonight are perfectly ordinary people. They're basically no different than I am, or the other men you know well. The point is that you should talk to them just as you'd talk to anyone else. You have a tremendously worthy purpose tonight, Alisa, one that has the potential to benefit the whole town. That makes yours and Paul's appearance at the meeting as important as any of theirs."

"But what if they don't take us seriously?" she said. "All day long I've been imagining how it will feel if they act like . . . well, like we're just a couple of *kids*."

Her father nodded, frowning slightly. "There's no use pretending that it's not a possibility," he said, "though you certainly mustn't go there *expecting* that kind of reception. There's only one way to prevent it—or to overcome it. *Be calm.* Whether or not you truly feel that way, you must act and speak as though you're absolutely controlled and confident. If any of them should behave as if you're not there for a responsible and admirable reason, yours and Paul's respectful, confident attitude will dispel any such notions, I feel sure."

"All right," she said, pleased to find that her voice was stronger already, "I'll do it. I'll pretend that it's no more difficult than giving an oral report in front of a class. I usually managed to hide my nervousness when I have to do that."

"That's the right attitude," her father replied with a warm smile. "I'd kind of like to be there tonight myself. You and Paul just might give somebody a whole new perception of teenagers."

Marty answered Paul's knock a few minutes later, and Paul picked him up, setting him on his shoulder. Marty grinned from ear to ear, while Darlene smiled shyly until Paul ruffled her hair and sat beside her on the sofa. Marty clambered down to sit at his other side.

"You look terrific, eighteen at least," Paul said, eyeing Alisa approvingly. "Ready to face the city fathers?"

"Not exactly," Alisa replied, "but I'll try not to let them know it."

"I was just a little nervous," he said. "Mom caught me trying to fix my tie. You should've seen the look on her face. She tried hard to keep from laughing, but she couldn't quite manage it."

"She *laughed* at you?" Alisa asked. Then: "But you're not wearing a tie."

"That's the point," he said. "When she finally quit laughing, she said, 'The tie is overkill, son, not a good idea. Surely you've been to enough business meetings with your father to know better than to be too anxious to impress them. They're just *boys* with gray hair, after all!'"

Alisa's father laughed, clearly enjoying Paul's story and his mimicry of his mother's manner. But it disturbed Alisa. Was Paul making fun of his mother?

Then, seeing her discomfort, Paul said, "I forgot; you haven't met my mother. You'd have to know her to understand. She's a little . . . different, but she's okay."

Just as they were preparing to leave, Marty caught Alisa's hand. "I forgot to tell you that my teacher said we can bring our plants home tomorrow. Will you help me set it out?"

"Sure," she told him. "We'll do it when we all get home from school."

"I don't understand," Alisa said when they were in Paul's car, "about your mother. I guess what I mean is that I can't figure out how *you* feel about her. Sometimes you seem angry, and then other times you tease."

Paul looked her way, and a wrinkle appeared be-

117

tween his heavy dark brows as he considered her comment. Then he began to speak slowly, as though selecting his words with great care.

"A couple of weeks ago I was angry," he said. "I've been angry for a long time, I guess. I suppose I always knew that it was because of the divorce."

"Are you saying that you felt it was your mother's fault?" she asked, cautious about asking so personal a question.

"I did feel that way, but lately I've been thinking it over a little more objectively. I haven't seen much of my dad since we came back here to live, and I'm beginning to think that's partly why I've been so hard on Mom. I mean, it was hard to blame Dad, see, when I'd just see him on weekends, and then not nearly that often after we moved from Chicago. When I visited Dad, we always had a great time. He'd take me places, even to work with him. But it never lasted long enough. I haven't figured it all out yet, but . . ." He paused, laughing at himself, she felt sure. "I'll just put it this way," he finally said, still smiling. "In the last week or two my mother has gotten quite a bit more lovable. She's starting to grow up, see?"

Alisa only smiled in response, but she thought perhaps she really did see, now. For during the past few days Paul had seldom shown any evidence of the dark moodiness that had hovered about him for so long, even disturbing her when she'd met him in the halls at school, before she actually knew him.

It was odd, too, that in only a week or so he had become so much more relaxed. He smiled easily now, and his manner was more often humorous and lighthearted than heavy and silent. What was causing him to change so quickly? she wondered. Whatever it was, she was glad. They were spending so much time together now, becoming close friends without a hint of romance. She was glad of that, too; she couldn't handle even the smallest skirmish in the age-old battle of the sexes the way things had been going. Of that much she was absolutely certain!

Then they were there, in front of the fine conference room the savings and loan had built as a community meeting place. Alisa had never been inside the room before. She wasn't exactly looking forward to it.

However, once they were inside, it wasn't terribly imposing. The thick carpet felt luxurious, and the soft, warm beige walls gently absorbed the light from a beautiful, sparkling chandelier, the only really striking thing in the room.

Several men were already seated around the oval table, and for a moment she felt at a loss, wondering whether she should take one of the empty chairs.

Then she became aware of a friendly, welcoming face. Arthur McLeary beamed at her from across the table, evidently as much at ease there as he had been in his own flower shop.

"Well, if it isn't Alisa Wilson," he said with a warm smile. "I knew we were expecting some young folks, but I didn't know it was you. Have a seat, young lady, and introduce your friend."

Grateful for the unexpected welcome and pleased

that he had remembered her, Alisa stepped forward and took the chair that Paul had been quick to draw out for her. "My friend is Paul Heyser," she said. "We're both juniors at Rutland High."

The men went through a few formalities then, giving Alisa and Paul a few minutes to become a bit more comfortable in the unfamiliar atmosphere. But all too soon they turned their attention to the visitors. Alisa felt that the eyes of all the men were on her.

"Alisa and Paul, all of us want to tell you that we appreciate your interest in the betterment of our city," Mayor Bradshaw said, "but we aren't too clear about what you have in mind. Would one of you like to explain your petition?"

They had planned that she would speak first if they had a choice, and Alisa drew a deep breath. Although none of the men had stood to speak, she felt that standing might give her courage, so she pushed her chair backward and stood on shaky legs. For some reason her speech teacher's advice from the previous year came to her aid, and she glanced around at each of the men, presumably to gain eye contact but more accurately to give her a moment to compose herself. Then she had to speak.

"Paul's and my English teacher, Mister Reed, challenged us to try to do something to benefit our society," she said, pleased that the trembling she felt inside didn't disclose itself too obviously in her voice. "Paul and I have determined to accept that challenge," she went on, "but we would like all of you to understand that we do this on our own; we take the responsibility for our actions. Mister Reed gave us the original inspiration, but this is not actually a school-sponsored project.''

''What we intend to do,'' she went on with more courage, ''is to get the people of South Rutland as interested as we are in cleaning up that part of town, improving the whole general appearance. We don't know how far we'll be able to go, how successful we might be, but already a lot of people are excited enough that they have scheduled a meeting for tomorrow night to plan a course of action.

''What we want to achieve is this: We want to get the people to clean up their yards and do as much as they can afford toward making repairs on their homes. We want to help them plant flowers and do other things to brighten the whole south side. We are convinced that if we can do this, the people will be happier, pleased with their accomplishments, and more interested in all aspects of city management. And we believe that all of Rutland will be better because of it.''

Well, she'd gotten through it, but her knees were shaking so that she barely trusted herself to move. ''That is our plan, and those are our goals,'' she said. ''Paul will discuss this in more detail if you will give us a few more minutes of your time.''

Then she made it into her chair, somehow without falling onto the floor, and hooked her fingertips together so the man seated on her left would not see how they trembled. Then she looked up at Paul, though at first she could barely see him.

He spoke magnificently, asking the ''acknowledged leaders of the city'' to consider any opportunity to assist and encourage their efforts.

"We will be very glad for anything you might do," he said in conclusion, "except for what I suppose I must call a 'condition.' We want the *people* to make all the plans and carry them out, hopefully with some assistance from the city government and possibly service agencies. But we insist that all public acknowledgment of credit for any accomplishments go to the residents themselves. It must be this way; otherwise, our real purpose would be defeated.

"Alisa and I thank you for listening. If you have any questions, we'll try to answer them. Then we will leave you to continue with your responsibilities."

Paul sat, and she wondered whether he felt as odd and stunned as she did because of how good they had both sounded. The men talked quietly among themselves for a moment, and then a tall, thin man with blondish-gray hair spoke up.

"I'll tell you what I think," the man said. "These two kids deserve a lot of appreciation for being so interested in improving our city. It isn't every day that teenagers take such an interest." He smiled about him then, and several of the men expressed agreement.

"But we can't devote much attention to this project right now," another man said. "Maybe later on in the summer. Right now we've got to concentrate on getting some industry in this town. Put the people to work first, I say. *Then* let 'em worry about cleaning up their yards!"

Alisa seethed. How could anyone be so crude?

The man sounded as if he were speaking of robots instead of fellow citizens.

"Now, Ed, settle down," the man next to him said. "We can help these kids some way, surely. That city ordinance against keeping unlicensed automobiles, for instance. We've never really followed through on that. We could start enforcing it real strictly. It wouldn't cost the city a dime, and they'd get rid of all those junk cars in a hurry or pay for the city to tow 'em to a junkyard. That would do a lot to help these kids out!"

Without knowing when she had moved, Alisa found herself on her feet. "You're talking about *punishing* people, about *forcing* them," she cried. "Didn't you understand what Paul just said? We've come to ask you to *help* us, not to undermine what we've already gotten started!"

Then she caught the signals from Arthur McLeary, seated across from her, and sat down again, hoping she hadn't ruined whatever chance they might have had.

Mr. McLeary stood. "We're mighty proud of what you're trying to do," he said seriously, with no hint of joking or teasing in his voice or manner. "If you will give us a few days to think it over, I'm sure we'll find some way to help you. To try is the least we can do. And I promise you, Alisa—" He looked directly at her. "—whether or not we find a way to help, we will *not* get in your way!"

Impressed by the happy, jolly man's suddenly authoritative and businesslike manner, Alisa got to her feet along with Paul. "Thank you," they said at the same time. The men nodded and thanked them in return, then grew silent as they walked out of the room.

Chapter Eighteen

THE CITY COUNCIL meeting remained in Alisa's thoughts all through the day at school on Friday. Although she and Paul had handled it better than they had expected, the reaction of the men troubled and disappointed her, especially the business about forcing people to do part of what she and Paul were trying to inspire them to do for themselves. What if they actually did start to enforce that ordinance? The effect was guaranteed to be disastrous.

Mr. McLeary had promised to help or at least, as she had understood him, to keep the men from hindering their efforts. But how much influence did he actually have? At the meeting she had seen a surprisingly impressive side to the man, but she couldn't help wondering whether he could actually do anything.

"I wouldn't worry about it if I were you," her father had said when she had told him about the meeting. "It's true that I don't know much about Art McLeary except what I remember from high school, and that's mostly how popular he was as a fun-loving clown. But he was capable of being serious even then. He wasn't always a clown, because

125

he was in some honors math and science classes with me.''

"Then you think maybe they'll listen to him?"

"I can't say for sure, of course," her father had replied, "but if he said they wouldn't get in your way, I suspect he'll be able to back it up."

She had felt a little better then, but still uncomfortable. She wished that she and Paul hadn't gone to the meeting at all.

The day dragged, and she was glad when seventh period came at last. Soon she would be able to go home.

But then there was the other meeting she had promised to attend. And they certainly didn't have any good news to pass along, as they had hoped.

Mr. Reed asked them to remain briefly after class; he wanted to know what had happened the night before. When they told him, he was obviously troubled but not discouraged. As he expressed his satisfaction with their work so far, the principal's secretary came rushing in.

"Oh, so you *are* still here," she said to Alisa, handing her a slip of paper. "I took this message for you half an hour ago. Then we were so overwhelmed with all sorts of details in the office, I forgot to bring it to you."

Alisa unfolded the paper and read it aloud: "Alisa Wilson, stop by the flower shop on your way home if you possibly can. Art McLeary."

"You'd better go," Mr. Reed said. "Maybe he will have some encouraging information for you, after all. If he does, it'll help at the meeting tonight. And by the way, I think I'll drop in tonight just to listen.''

They had agreed that Paul would drive Alisa home every day while there was so much to do on the project. She was grateful, although she had enjoyed the quiet walk most of the time. But Paul's driving her did save time and energy, and she surely needed that.

Mr. McLeary met them at the door, again the jolly, cheerful man she had first met. Just going into the wonderful flower shop gave Alisa's spirits a lift, but she was dying to know why he had asked them to come.

''You two young'uns come right on in here and breathe some real springtime,'' he said, leading them through the rows of breathtaking color and scent toward a cluttered desk that apparently served as an office. ''After a week of being shut up in classrooms, I expect you could use a little brightness, huh?'' His round, glowing face was such a picture of joy that Alisa suspected that his presence alone would have cheered her.

''I just figured out who your daddy is,'' he went on as he shuffled through an untidy stack of papers. ''I knew Bernard Wilson right well back when we were kids. Didn't know your mama then, but I've met her since. She's a fine lady who understands the benefits of flowers. And how's your daddy doing, anyway? I've been meaning to come by and see him, and doggone it, I'm *going* to, soon as I can find a spare minute. Oh, yes, *here* it is,'' he said without pausing for a reply. ''Have a look at this.'' He held a sheet of paper toward her and turned to Paul. "Knew your folks, too," he was saying. "Your mama was the prettiest girl in school, and by golly, she still is! Saw her just a couple of days ago, and she . . ."

Alisa studied the paper, puzzled at the meaning, while Mr. McLeary talked on. Didn't the man ever run down?

The logo at the top of the sheet was simple. It said "McLeary's Flowers." A border of tiny blossoms and leaved vines encircled the words. The only other thing on the sheet was a list of addresses. There were seven, in different cities, including the address in Rutland. What did it mean? Why had he shown it to her? She waited, and in a moment he turned back to her.

"Those are my flower shops," he said simply, with pride that wasn't boastful.

She was surprised; she had assumed that McLeary's Flowers was only a single store. But why was he showing her the list of his seven stores?

"Every spring there are various plants that have to be thrown out," he said then, suddenly the serious businessman. "Some are annuals and wouldn't be worth anything once they've bloomed, but there's always a lot of others—even the azaleas, some of them—that wouldn't thrive till next spring in pots, but they'd do fine if they were put out properly."

"You two were impressive last night," he went on. "It was clear to me that you were dead serious about what you're doing. And then today I saw a couple of those posters. And as if that wasn't enough, I've had two ladies in the shop today, buying flowers and talkin' about your meetin' tonight.

"So I got to thinking. Why throw out all those plants and things when they could be put to good use right here in my own hometown? Now, here's what I've come up with: I've got a truck, keeps on the move from one store to another, delivering new stock, shifting stuff from a store that's overstocked on an item to another store that's running short of the same thing. See what I mean? And what I did was, I got hold of my driver and told him to pick up all the stuff that looks to be throwaways from all the stores and bring all of it here. Then we'll just give it away to the folks in South Rutland. Now, you've gotta understand that these plants are perfectly good ones; they're just things that we judge won't make it unless they're taken out of the flowerpots and set in the ground."

Utterly amazed, Alisa and Paul stared at one another and at Mr. McLeary, who still didn't give them time to speak.

"Only problem is," he went on, "that I can't keep them here for more'n a day. There's just no room. And if folks are real interested, if there's a crowd, I'm gonna need some help. The truck'll be here next Tuesday. Now, do you reckon you could tell the folks about the free flowers tonight and make sure they know they've *gotta* get them on Tuesday, and get me some help, too?"

All they could do at first was smile and nod foolishly. "We sure can do all that," Paul finally said. "It's just a terrific thing for you to do! But won't that—giving flowers away, free of charge, I mean—

won't it kind of eliminate your profits? Even if they are things you'd have to dispose of, if people get them free, won't that stop them from buying other flowers?''

Mr. McLeary chuckled. ''You've gotta understand human nature, son,'' he said. ''I thought up this plan on account of you two and what you're doing, but if I'd been thinkin' like a businessman, I'd have done this every year in this store. The fact is, I can't lose. I don't sell too many flowers to South Rutland folks. Most of my flower customers come from the north side. The South Rutland folks mostly buy garden seeds and plants. And after this, do you reckon a single *one* of 'em will buy their garden stuff anywhere but here? They sure won't; you can take that to the bank. Why, son, I'll be takin' in profits for the next five years on account of this one little thing. Don't you know about the law of compensation yet? Anything you do good in this world, without greedy intentions, it'll come back to you doubled and doubled again!''

''There's just one more thing,'' he said, ''and then I'll let you two get on about your business. After you left last night, I told 'em a thing or two. You don't have to worry about the city enforcing that ordinance. I even sort of suggested to the mayor after the meetin' was over that it'd be a good investment in public relations if the city hauled all the junk cars and other big things like that away at no charge. Now, that's not been decided, understand, so you'd better not mention it to anybody yet, but I kind of think it will happen. You see, I can be just a wee bit devious when I need to. Before we were through talkin', I had Mayor Bradshaw thinkin' the whole thing was *his* idea!''

Because of the unplanned stop at the flower shop, everything had to be rushed at home. While she peeled potatoes for supper, Marty came to Alisa, proudly holding up the milk carton containing the bean plant.

"Here's my happiness plant," he said. "Don't you think it's pretty, Alisa?"

"Very pretty," Alisa replied, admiring it briefly.

"When can we set it out in the backyard?" he inquired, his big eyes wide and eager for her attention.

"I can't help you right now, Marty," she said. "I have to fix supper first. I don't have much time."

"*After* supper, then?"

"Sure, I guess so. After supper," she agreed. "But you'd better put it in your room for now so it won't get dropped or spilled."

He took his happiness plant away then, and she hurried to put the chops in the oven. Her father came in and made the salad while Darlene set the table. While they worked, Alisa reported on her and Paul's visit with Art McLeary.

"That's a fine thing he's doing," her father said, "and if he really can get the city to haul junk, it will give everybody a break. I wonder if I could help him next Tuesday, after I get back from my classes."

"Sure, why not?" Alisa said. "I'll tell him to expect you."

"I hope you don't have anything planned for tomorrow morning," her father said. "Meredith called, and I thought we'd drive up there."

"Oh, *good*!" Darlene cried. "Do you think Mama will get to come home with us?"

"Not yet," her father said gently, "but it won't be much longer now. At least one week. Possibly two. Doctor Marshall hasn't promised yet."

Before they had finished the dishes, Paul came to take Alisa to the block supervisors' meeting. She felt harried and too rushed, and although a part of her was eager to see what would happen, another part wanted nothing more than to crawl into bed and hide from the world.

She wasn't *ready*, but she had managed to shower and change, and before she knew it, they were in the basement of the Baptist church.

There weren't too many people, only fifteen or so adults and a few children, but the room felt crowded to Alisa. Then, when they had taken seats and settled down, Mrs. Carter said, "Alisa, somebody's going to have to get things started, and I reckon it ought to be you."

She had been afraid it would happen that way, and she got to her feet reluctantly. She was not at all prepared. What was she going to say? What was she even *doing* here, a sixteen-year-old trying to lead a group of adults in a half-formed plan that she'd probably had no business starting in the first place?

"I'm not sure what we ought to do tonight," she said. "I suppose the first thing is to see whether we have someone willing to supervise the improvements on each block. I guess we need . . . I wish we had a map.''

"I've got one right here, drew it up myself," a man she recognized as Ralph Carner said, standing to unfold a large sheet of white paper. He brought it forward and thumbtacked it to the wall behind Alisa, who studied it. She was delighted to see that not only were the streets clearly labeled, but people's names were written on several blocks.

"Those are the names of the block volunteers," Mr. Carner said. "And there's a few more since we got here, too. I'll call them out if you want to write them on the map."

When they were finished, there were only four blocks with no names.

"What I'd like to know," someone said, "is just what it's going to mean to be a block supervisor."

Alisa thought fast. She and Paul had discussed it, but maybe not as thoroughly as they should have.

"I think the main responsibility is going to be to encourage everyone, to help them get information and help. There will be some ladies who live alone, and they won't be able to, say, replace a window screen. They'll need to tell the block supervisor, then the supervisor will try to find someone who's able and willing to do that job. And some people won't know much about planting flowers. Those people will need the advice of someone who knows about such things, like Mrs. Carter." Here she glanced at Mrs. Carter, to find her beaming with pride and nodding her agreement.

"Then the supervisor's job will be to kind of

arrange for everyone to . . . uh, swap talents,"
someone said. "That's a great idea!"

Then she told them about Mr. McLeary and the
flowers, and the room erupted in exclamations of
delight. It was every bit as good as Christmas.

On it went. Someone suggested a prize for the
best improvement, and someone else volunteered
to take before and after Polaroid pictures of every
house for judging purposes. A woman who worked
at a photo processing shop felt sure that her employer would donate the film or at least let them
have it at cost.

Having their house painted or a new door or some
similar thing would be a good prize, someone said.
Ralph Carner said he would try to get his employer
to donate those things. He knew for a fact that there
were several cans of a discontinued brand of paint
in the storeroom at Rutland Building Supplies,
along with several other items.

Alisa could hardly believe it, the marvelous, infectious excitement and eagerness surrounding her.
She was on a cloud of jubilation, and she could see
by the sparkle in Paul's eyes that he felt the same
way.

They prepared to leave, with the people chatting
in groups that shifted here and there, making plans
and joking among themselves. Then, in a chair near
the door, they saw Mr. Reed. Alisa had forgotten
that he had said he would be there, and she hadn't
seen him come in. He wore a smile that could have
lighted the whole room.

"Well, what do you think, Mister Reed?" Paul
asked proudly.

"What can I say? It's as good as *done* already," Mr. Reed replied. "Do you two realize the magnitude of what you have achieved? I really can't find the words to tell you. Just don't let up. You've got to stay involved awhile longer. You've got to see it finished!"

Chapter Nineteen

ON THEIR WAY into the city on Saturday morning, neither her father nor Marty or Darlene showed any signs of the tension of the earlier visit, but Alisa couldn't seem to share their eagerness and good cheer. It wasn't that she wasn't anxious to see her mother, not at all. Every day the longing for her mother's presence, her warmth, her wisdom and gentleness grew stronger in Alisa's heart. At times she felt that she couldn't bear her mother's absence another day, and when she watched Marty and Darlene absorbed in play or giving their full attention to a movie or some other distraction, she wondered whether they had been able to completely forget that their mother wasn't there for those few moments.

She could almost hope it was true, for them. While even momentary forgetting seemed unforgivable, at least for someone as old as she, Alisa could envy the younger children the single-minded concentration that appeared to give them rest from missing their mother. But for her, thoughts of her mother seemed to affect everything she did, every choice she made, the things she thought about and the things she spoke about.

Oh, how she wanted her mother to come home! Only she wanted to feel free of the unrelenting fear that it would happen again. She didn't think she could bear it again, the terror that exploded inside her at every little thing—a headache, a moment of melancholy, a few minutes of thoughtful silence—that might possibly be a symptom of the recurrence of that devastating, all-encompassing depression. Was there never to be a way to be *certain*?

"Alisa, listen!"

Her father nodded toward the radio. Apparently he had spoken to her more than once, for she caught only the end of the announcement: ". . . and that's what's happening in South Rutland, a *massive* cleanup campaign. Everyone is urged to get involved, and all of us at the radio station want to say, 'Cheers for the residents of South Rutland!' "

"Who's responsible for the announcement?" her father asked. "It's great!"

Alisa shook her head, thoroughly puzzled. "I have no idea," she said, "but you're right; it sounded good. I don't think Paul did it, or he would have told me. It must have been someone who was at the meeting last night."

"It's what you've been hoping for, then," he replied. "The people are shouldering the responsibilities, it appears. You and Paul should be very proud, Alisa."

He was absolutely right, of course; she should be pleased that it was working out so well, so much better than she had even dared to hope, as a matter of fact. And she was glad. She was. The funny little hollow feeling inside that reminded her for some reason of the time she hadn't been invited to MaryLee Watkins's eighth birthday party was surely just a result of all the things she couldn't quit worrying about; that was all it was.

Her mother met them in the hall, again dressed cheerfully and attractively. She hugged them all over and over, but she seemed better able to restrain the tears of emotion this time. And she laughed more easily, more like she'd always done before. She wanted to hear about all their activities, of course, beginning with her husband's progress in college.

"To tell you the truth, Meredith, it reminds me of when I was a kid. There are all these reading assignments and writing assignments, and there are times when I'd rather chuck the books and go out and play. Then I think how embarrassing it would be for you and the kids to see a D on my report card, and that inspires me to get back to work!"

Her gay laughter at his comparison was the thing Alisa had been looking for in her mother without fully realizing it until that moment; her actual, spontaneous sense of humor was definitely coming back! That was one of the facets of her mother's personality that caused people to respond to her with such warmth and trust. But peculiarly, the sense of humor seemed to be the first thing that had begun to dissolve each time. But why was she thinking of such things now?

"Your father told me on the phone about the fantastic project you've been working on, sweetheart," Meredith said then. "Tell me everything about it! It sounded so exciting; I can hardly wait to see, but for now, tell me!"

So she described the project as well as she could without monopolizing all the visiting time, and it was obvious that her mother was delighted and proud of her eldest daughter. "I wish I could've been there to help you," she said, "but I'll still get to help some. Surely it won't be all over with before I come home. But tell me now—what else is new?"

"Alisa's got a boyfriend, that's what else," Darlene said, giggling. "He's real nice and his name's Paul and he has a blue car and he brings Alisa home *every day*. And I wish I could have a boyfriend, too, so I wouldn't have to walk so far!"

That had to be clarified a bit, naturally. When it had been settled and the troubled look had gone from her mother's eyes, she turned to Marty.

"I've been wondering about your happiness plant," she told him. "Have you brought it home yet?"

His wide eyes turned briefly and reproachfully onto Alisa, and she groaned. She had forgotten! How could she have forgotten something that was so important to Marty? Her mother would *never* have forgotten, not *that*.

"I brought it home yesterday," Marty told his mother. "It's a real good plant, and it has four leaves now instead of just two! Alisa was s'posed to help me set it out yesterday, but she had to go to that meeting right after supper, so it's still just setting there on my dresser."

"We'll do it the very minute after we get back home, Marty," Alisa said. "I *promise*, no matter what else needs to be done!"

"Honey, don't take it so seriously," her mother urged her. "My goodness, you can't possibly remember *everything*. Even a superwoman is bound to forget something now and then."

She did not forget again, and as soon as they were at home, she helped Marty dig up a place for his precious plant. Then he carried it proudly out to the backyard, and Darlene and their father watched solemnly while Marty and Alisa set it into the dirt and then watered it.

The moment they came back inside, the phone rang. It was Paul.

"Let's go and talk to some of the people this afternoon," he said. "That way we'll sort of be keeping in touch, and—"

"Not today, Paul," Alisa replied. "Thanks for calling, but it's time I stayed home for a while . . . tomorrow, too. I've been neglecting my family, and I can't do that anymore."

"Well, okay," Paul said. "See you Monday morning, then?"

"Sure. Monday morning," Alisa replied. "See you."

"What was that about?" her father asked when she left the telephone. "I didn't mean to eavesdrop, but I heard you say something about neglecting us. Now, that simply is not true, Alisa. If there's some reason why you didn't want to see Paul, fine. But if you really meant that comment about neglecting us, you'd better think it over a little more carefully. I will *not* have you thinking that way; do you hear?''

''I hear,'' Alisa said, swallowing back a sudden ridiculous urge to cry. ''Paul and I didn't need to do anything today, anyway. I just want to stay home for a while. Besides, I don't think the project would break down now even if I didn't give it another thought. It's gathering momentum now. It'll work out with or without me.''

Her father watched her closely. ''Does that mean you're quitting?'' he asked quietly.

''Well, no,'' she said. ''I'm not quitting. There's still the flowers at McLeary's, and . . . I was just thinking out loud, Dad.''

''That's good,'' he said, ''because if you should decide to drop out now, after all the . . . but never mind. You aren't thinking about that, so everything's fine, right?''

''Right,'' she said, leaving him. She didn't feel much like talking, and there was lunch to fix.

Chapter Twenty

On Monday evening, when they had finished their meal, their father said, "Kids, I have some wonderful news for you. On Saturday morning I'll be going into the city—and I'll bring your mother back with me!"

"Oh, boy, I can't wait!" Marty cried, unable to sit still in his excitement. "How long is it till Saturday, Alisa? I still get the days mixed up sometimes."

Alisa restrained her own elation to answer him. She held up five fingers. "It's five days, Marty," she said, "or five nights. The time will pass quickly; you'll see."

Darlene's eyes had brimmed with tears at the news, but she brushed the tears away with her fingers. "Mama's been gone a long time," she said. "I hope she never has to go to that old hospital again. I just can't *stand* it when Mama's not here!"

Her tiny voice sounded so desolate, so pain-filled that it was all Alisa could do to keep her own tears in check. "All of us feel that way, Darlene," she said. "There's just no way that we can know for certain; nobody can promise that Mom won't ever have to go back. But we do think she's a lot better. Maybe she won't get sick again.''

"You kids have been wonderful," their father said. "You've been as strong and brave as any hero could have been, and I wish I could tell you how much I love you all. I'm very, very proud of you."

"Is five days long enough for us to finish our surprises?" Marty asked. "We made some big butterflies already, and we're going to hang them out on the porch. But we haven't even started the welcome-home sign."

"It'll be long enough, I think," Alisa said, "but you'll have to work on it a little while every night. Maybe you should get started while I do the dishes."

"But you've gotta help us make the letters straight," Darlene said.

"Bring me the paper, kids, and a ruler," their father said. "I'll help with the letters. Alisa already has enough to do."

It was true enough, but Alisa also felt glad to have the kitchen to herself for a little while. For that she would gladly do the dishes by herself.

Her mother would be home on Saturday! She felt light, excited; she wanted to cry and sing and laugh. Their lives would get back to normal; their mother's bubbling laughter would ring through the house again. A week from today she would come home from school to hear that delightful voice singing along with the radio; her parents would sit snuggled close on the sofa in the evenings, and the mornings would be leisurely and cheerful instead of rushed and frantic. And when she felt sad or troubled, she'd have the warmth of her mother's comforting embrace and gentle wisdom.

For a little while she simply stood there, her hands in the soapy water, basking in the joyous visions of what it would be like to have her mother home again. It was heavenly; it was pure loveliness!

Then, though she began furiously scrubbing the dishes, willing herself to banish her thoughts, they came scurrying like ants. You've been angry, Alisa. You've been embarrassed; you knew it was wrong, but you couldn't stop it. You were angry at the most perfect mother in the world! You were *ashamed* of her sometimes because of her illness, and when you felt guilty, you tried to blame those awful feelings on others. But they were in *your* mind, Alisa. And you never figured out how to send those thoughts away, did you? So they must still be lurking somewhere, mustn't they? So how are you going to feel when your mother holds you in her arms to comfort your silly little pains, Alisa? You thought you felt guilt before this, but you haven't felt *anything* yet, Alisa.

"Mister Reed," she said after the dismissal bell on Tuesday, "Could you stay for a minute, please? I'd like to talk to you. Only it's pretty personal. . . ."

He nodded. "Paul's been taking you home," he said. "Have you mentioned this to him?"

"No. I mean, I didn't know. Maybe I'd better wait. . . ."

"If you wouldn't mind riding with me, I'll take

you home," Mr. Reed said. "I have to go that direction anyway. I'll tell Paul."

He spoke briefly with Paul, and she didn't even wonder what he had said. She had barely spoken to him all day long, but then, she'd barely spoken to anyone.

"I don't want to talk about this at all," she confessed when they were alone in the room. "It's just that my mother's coming home on Saturday, and I've got to get some things figured out before then."

"Is it . . . is there something that's happened while she's been away?" Mr. Reed asked. "Something that you're worried about her learning about?"

Alisa shook her head. "Only inside my mind," she said. "I'm all mixed up about some things. Well . . . mostly about the fact that my mother's been in a . . . psychiatric ward."

"Are you telling me that you've felt embarrassed about that?" Mr. Reed asked.

She nodded. "Embarrassed. Angry. Ashamed. Guilty. Mister Reed, I love my mother. She's not just good, she's practically *perfect*. And I can't stand it that I've been thinking things. . . . I feel disloyal, a traitor. Only, I don't know what to do about it. I know that if I told Mom how I've been feeling, she'd forgive me. But that's not enough. I won't ever forget that those things were in my mind. What am I going to do? I'm not very good at talking about personal stuff; it embarrasses me. But she's coming home on Saturday. And I can hardly wait. Only . . ."

Mr. Reed nodded thoughtfully. Then he said,

"Alisa, I know this won't help you very much, but my first thought is to be glad you're living in this era instead of, say, fifty or a hundred years ago. There isn't nearly so much prejudice about such things as there once was. But your problem is that many people still can't feel comfortable about it. Hardly anyone is crude enough to be deliberately cruel. In fact, I'd say most people want to be kind and understanding, but they don't know how to express their feelings. So they say the wrong things or they say nothing at all, which is probably even worse."

She knew that Mr. Reed had a deeper than average perception of things, a special awareness of the hows and whys of human behavior and attitudes. Still, she was surprised that he had so immediately put a finger on one of the most disturbing issues. But it was the same thing she'd been telling herself all along, and it hadn't helped.

"The thing is," she said, "that *I* knew better. I've been sort of blaming my own problems on the way other people have behaved, and it's no solution. I *knew* it was wrong to feel anything except concern for my mother's health. And most of the time I've been able to do all right. But sometimes . . . Mister Reed, I don't think I'm going to feel right until I can find a way to *un*do those bad thoughts, to erase them. And that pretty much means that I'll never feel right."

"It's not that hopeless," he said gently. "Remember what I said the other day about solving problems—that you can't find a solution until you've come to understand the cause? I think that's all you need, Alisa. I feel sure that you'll be fine as soon as you discover the real reasons for your negative feelings. But I'm not sure that I'm the right person to help you. I'll say this much, though. I suspect that you're on the right track when you refuse to put the blame for your discomfort on the unsupportive reactions of other people. On the other hand, you must stop blaming yourself. Blame implies responsibility, and the sole responsibility for what troubles you absolutely does not rest on the degree of your own goodness, or knowledge, or fairness. This much I know, although I don't know how to help you to find the deeper cause. Put all thought of modesty aside, Alisa, and you'll be able to see the truth—that you *are* a good, fair, knowledgeable person. My point is that there's no basic flaw in your character. The cause lies somewhere else, and I believe that Mrs. Birnam could help you recognize it. Has it occurred to you to talk with her?''

Alisa nodded. ''Paul mentioned it one day, but for some reason I don't feel real sure of myself with her. I mean, I know she's real nice, and she does know an awful lot. Her advice about the project was exactly right. I just . . . I guess I just felt that I knew you better.''

''Talk to her, Alisa,'' Mr. Reed encouraged. ''Mrs. Birnam knows more about what motivates human behavior than anyone I've ever met. And what better way to know someone than to ask for his help? To ask a few fellow human being to help us with his special skills or knowledge is the highest compliment we can pay. And Alisa, you *can* trust her. Will you at least consider talking to her? I feel that I've let you down somewhat, and I truly want you to feel better about all this.''

"I'll think about it," Alisa promised. "Probably I'll talk to her. Thank you, Mister Reed.''

She decided to walk home, after all. The day was beautiful and warm and fresh. Maybe it would be good to walk.

And it was. People waved and greeted her from their yards and vegetable gardens, and practically everyone seemed cheerful. They were enjoying the fine day and enjoying their work, too, it appeared. A part of her felt as elated as they; it was just that one dark spot haunted her so.

At the flower shop Mr. McLeary looked harried, but not in a negative way. He was enjoying the rush and flow of people who had come to select flowers and bushes and such from the flat wooden platforms outside, where they'd been unloaded from the truck. Her father was there, too, along with Paul, who had even gone to pick up Marty and Darlene so they wouldn't be at home alone.

Seeing that, she almost cried. She had known her father would be at the flower shop, and she'd forgotten that if she didn't come straight home, her brother and sister would be there by themselves. How could she have been so careless? It was good that her mother would soon be home, because she was losing her concentration or something.

Her father greeted her happily, but he was busy with the people, indicating the different kinds of plants and encouraging them to take what they wanted for their own yards. Marty and Darlene were working, too, helping to carry flowerpots to cars and such.

She saw several people whom she had met at the block supervisors' meeting, and they greeted her with such warmth, such affection, that she was again almost moved to tears. Everyone seemed so happy, laughing and talking among themselves as they might have done at a neighborhood barbecue. If only they could always be so full of cheer and optimism! If only there would be no ugly surprises in any of their futures, no perverse power that would jerk them off their feet for no reason and alter their lives forever.

The week dragged, and Alisa didn't speak to Mrs. Birnam. On Thursday evening Marty and Darlene proudly displayed the welcome-home banner they had made by stapling sheets of bright construction paper together and coloring the letters with loving care, and she and her father admired their work, assuring them that it was exactly, ideally right.

Paul had driven her home again, and he stayed for supper. He was full of energy and good spirits, and she tried to match his mood, afraid that he wasn't fooled by the part that was forced. She felt awfully glad for Paul. Something had changed him; working on the project, maybe. Whatever it was, she was truly, deeply pleased.

Then Marty, who had gone outside, came in with tears streaming. Hurrying to take him into her arms, Alisa couldn't make out what the problem was for a moment. He tried to talk through his tears, and at last he succeeded.

"My happiness plant—it's all broke," he sobbed. "I went to see, because it was for Mama 'specially, and this morning it had six leaves. But it's all broke, and now it's not any good!"

Feeling his heartache, Alisa held him close for a moment. She didn't know what to say to help him. Then Paul spoke up. "Let's go out and have a look," he said. "Maybe it isn't ruined, Marty. Some of the flowers were broken off today, too, but Mister McLeary showed me that they might still grow and make new flowers."

So they went out into the near dusk, and the bean plant truly was, as Marty had said, broken. Four of the six leaves were still there, but the top two were missing. "It was a rabbit, Marty," his father said after looking around. "A rabbit bit it off. But I don't really think it's ruined."

"It isn't," Paul said after examining the plant. "According to Mister McLeary, as along as these leaves are still here, your happiness plant should still grow. But we're going to have to spray it with something to keep the rabbit from eating any more leaves."

All it took was a telephone call to Mr. McLeary for advice, and in a little while the bean plant was covered with a fine dusting of powder that he assured them would keep the rabbit away.

Marty's tears were dried, and he was happy again, but Alisa couldn't help wondering. Was the partial destruction of her little brother's happiness plant an omen?

Chapter Twenty-one

ON FRIDAY, WHILE she was making sandwiches and soup for their supper, the phone rang. A moment later her father called out, "It's for you, Alisa. It's Mayor Bradshaw."

Curious and a bit nervous, Alisa went to the telephone. What could Mayor Bradshaw possibly want with her?

"I suppose you've seen the paper," he said after they exchanged greetings.

"No, it hasn't been delivered yet, but it should be here any time," Alisa said. "Why?"

"You'll see," the mayor replied. "There's a pretty impressive article, and among other things, it mentioned a meeting for tonight in a Baptist church on the south side. Will you be at this meeting?"

"Yes, I plan to go," Alisa replied, growing increasingly nervous. Was he about to announce that the city would start enforcing the ordinance against keeping unlicensed cars?

"Then I'll appreciate it if you will make an announcement on behalf of Rutland's city council," Mayor Bradshaw said. "I'd first intended to send a

151

representative to the meeting, then I remembered your friend Paul's remarks. Anyway, we've been talking and trying to arrange something ever since you and Paul Heyser came to our meeting. And this evening, after I saw the newspaper, I felt the time was right. The council has decided that next Friday and Saturday we will put our city street equipment and employees to work. We will remove all junk cars and any other refuse that's too big for people to haul away for themselves, free of charge. No trash bags; just big things. Will you tell the people tonight?''

"I certainly will," Alisa exclaimed. "This is really wonderful news, Mister Bradshaw. I don't know how to thank you."

"Well, young lady, as you said at the city council meeting, it will be good for the whole town. But there is one more thing. Please also ask the people to see that everyone is ready so our men won't be wasting time and that they should be sure to take advantage of this opportunity. Because one month after the city does this hauling without charge, we *will* begin to strictly enforce the unlicensed automobile ordinance, and that will prevent the same situation from occurring again. All this will be published in the newspaper and on radio, of course, but I felt sure that you would enjoy making the first announcement."

"Oh, I will," Alisa said. "Thank you *so* much, Mister Bradshaw."

"There's just one *other* little detail," he said. "Just for fun, you might mention to your wily fox of a friend, Art McLeary, that he didn't fool me one bit but that I'm glad he got my attention, just the same.''

As soon as the conversation ended, Alisa went out to find the evening paper on the porch. She spread it open on the kitchen table where they could all see, and it *was* impressive. The whole center-fold had been devoted to an article, and there were at least a dozen photographs. Two photos featured Tuesday's activity at the flower shop, and Marty and Darlene squealed with delight to find them-selves in one of the pictures. There were pictures of people working in their yards and an especially unattractive shot of the overgrown lot near Mrs. Carter's house.

Her father read the article aloud. ''According to a spokesman of South Rutland, in a short time that part of our city will have a fresh new appearance. The residents have joined together in this remark-able effort, and already the changes are becoming apparent.''

It was a fine, encouraging article, and it pleased Alisa deeply. A wave of pride and satisfaction en-veloped her. She didn't know who was responsible for the news story, but it could not have been bet-ter. It featured the residents who were taking re-sponsibility and working, and they were heroes. She wondered whether Mrs. Birnam had seen the paper yet. When she did, she would see that her advice had certainly been followed.

Then she knew that it must have been Paul who had arranged for the article, and she smiled to her-self. She knew all too well that she had been some-what uncommunicative for a week. Perhaps tonight she would be able to relax. They had actually managed to do a pretty terrific thing, and she was proud. As Mr. Reed had suggested, when one put the hindering obligatory modesty aside, all that remained was truth—and the truth was right there in front of her, in the newspaper. They'd done well.

The first half of the block supervisors' meeting was a wonderful riot. They discussed the news story—Paul admitted to Alisa that he had arranged it on condition that the reporter would do it his way—and they cheered when Alisa made the announcement for the city council. Someone had indeed taken photos of the houses in the seventeen-block area and had mounted them neatly on poster board, with spaces to add the "after" pictures later.

"Let's set a deadline for the competition," someone said. "How about three weeks from today? We'll take the after pictures on the day before, and then . . . but who'll be the judge? It shouldn't be any of us."

"Or anyone else in Rutland," someone else added. "Since Paul and Alisa started this ball to rolling, maybe they could find us a judge from out of town."

"How about my father?" Paul asked. "He's in the construction business in Chicago, but he grew up here. He hasn't been back here in years, but he's coming for a visit. He'll be here then."

The suggestion suited everyone, and it was settled. Then Ralph Carner spoke up. "My boss said that he will supply our grand prize. He said he'll supply whatever home improvement materials the winner chooses from his store, up to a value of two hundred dollars!'' Again the crowd cheered.

More discussion of various details followed, and the meeting concluded with an agreement to meet again in three weeks for the announcement of the family judged to have achieved the greatest degree of improvement in the appearance of its home.

''We should celebrate some way, you know,'' Paul told her as they drove toward her house after the meeting. ''This project is the best—well, more like the second best thing that's ever happened to me, I think.''

''It's been great, all right,'' Alisa said. ''When I think about how unsure we were at first, especially me, I'm awfully glad we went on with it. Everyone seems so happy, so pleased with themselves and with each other. It's just about too remarkable to believe!''

''And your mom's coming home tomorrow, too,'' Paul said. ''That's going to be really good for all of you. I'm anxious to meet her myself. She couldn't be anything but really special, judging by the rest of her family.''

''She's special, all right,'' Alisa agreed. ''In some ways I think there's nobody else on earth as good. She's superkind, and generous, and interested in everything, and patient.''

''Like you, then,'' Paul said softly.

''Like me? You're joking,'' Alisa said, the sharpness in her voice surprising even herself. ''I didn't mean to snap at you,'' she added. ''That was a lovely compliment, more than you realize yet. Thank you.''

He stopped the car in her driveway and turned to lean against the door, facing her. ''Do you remember that first morning, when you were walking in the rain?'' he asked her.

''Of course; you gave me a ride,'' she said.

''Right. But what you gave me—that's what I remember,'' Paul said.

''But I didn't—''

''I was a mess,'' he said, interrupting her protest. ''I was mad at the whole wide world, and I was miserable. I'd been miserable for a long time. And there you were; you weren't disturbed or complaining about having to walk to school in the rain, like any other girl would've done; you didn't get mad or offended when I was hateful, and you even said we should get together again and talk. You were kind, and generous, and interested in me, and very patient—all the things you just said about your mother—and I thought you were the best human being I'd ever seen in my life.''

''But Paul, that wasn't anything special. I mean, I'm glad you felt that way, but . . . but . . .''

''The thing is, I didn't know the first thing about how terrific you were, not then,'' he went on as though he hadn't even heard her protests. ''When I came to your house and saw all the wonderful things you'd been doing every day, taking care of your family, being so great with Marty and Darlene especially . . . well, that's when I knew I had to change my attitude in a hurry. Alisa, before I met you, I was miserable. I didn't even like my own mother. And now I'm happy all the time, and my mom thinks you've got to be an angel sent from heaven just to straighten me out, and, well, I just wanted to tell you. Thank you.''

Glad to find her father and Marty absorbed in hearing Darlene's reading, Alisa went straight to her room. If she'd had to say a single word more then "Hi," she would've burst into tears.

The things Paul had said—they were just too much to assimilate all at once. His words weren't just compliments; they were more. They were *awards* . . . and she didn't deserve them.

Saturday morning came at last, and Alisa kept Marty and Darlene busy almost every minute cleaning the house, hanging their banner and their funny monstrous paper butterflies, decorating cookies, and raking the front yard. They couldn't stand the waiting until their mother came, and every time they were unoccupied for a moment, their impatience erupted in squabbles and bickering.

But the special, precious moment finally came. She heard their excited shouts from inside the house when they saw their father's car coming, and she hurried to join them.

There must have been a chill in the house all along, Alisa thought a few hours later, because the moment her mother entered the front door, everything seemed to take on a glow of warmth. There were no words that were truly adequate for expressing their joy, but there were hugs and kisses and more hugs. Marty and Darlene were delighted with

Meredith's pleasure over their banner and butterflies, and of course she had to see Marty's happiness plant right away, too.

But finally, gradually they relaxed, and Marty and Darlene went out to play. Alisa went to her room to give her parents a bit of privacy, but in a little while her mother came in and sat on her bed.

"I've missed you all more then ever this time," her mother said, "but one thing gave me a lot of comfort, and that was knowing that you would do everything possible to make things easier, especially for your little brother and sister. I'm terribly proud of you, Alisa, for the way you've taken care of things here. And as we drove through town earlier, I could see all the things that are happening because of you. I wanted to stop and tell everyone I saw, 'Alisa Wilson is my daughter; isn't she wonderful?' But your father said that everybody knows it already!"

"Oh, Mom," Alisa protested with a pleased smile, "I didn't do anything special. Mostly I just tried to do things the way I thought you would have done."

"You've given my compliment back to me doubled," her mother replied, "and that is the loveliest thing of all, for you to say that you've tried to imitate me. Well, we're going to be crying again in a minute if we don't stop this, but I had to try to tell you how glad I am about everything. I know it has been difficult for you, and your father says you haven't complained at all. I hope I never have to leave you this way again, Alisa. I . . . I'm sorry it happened this time, but now I truly believe it's over with at last.''

Chapter Twenty-two

THE DAYS PASSED in sunny happiness in South Rutland. All the junk cars and other debris disappeared from Alisa's street while she was in school. At almost every house, flowers bloomed, fresh paint brightened houses, broken things were fixed, lawns were mowed, and trees were trimmed. It was as if a doubled, intensified spring had come to South Rutland, and the vitality and freshness lifted Alisa's heart.

At home the evenings were fun and brimming with warmth and comfort. Her father looked happier every day. By midsummer he would be finished with college, and with her mother feeling marvelous, there was nothing more that she could wish for, at least nothing that anyone else could see.

It was only her own doubt that troubled Alisa. She found herself watching her mother too closely and listening for any evidence that might suggest a recurrence of her illness. Those times she felt ashamed, as if she should apologize to her mother for her lack of faith and trust. Every day she remembered the unpleasant thoughts and feelings of the preceding weeks and hoped those memories would fade and disappear. While Marty and Darlene quickly adjusted to having their mother back where she belonged, growing eager to go outside and play instead of staying close as they'd done the first few days, Alisa couldn't get enough of her mother's presence or her touch.

Only sometimes, when she sought her mother's hugs, a wave of guilt intervened, dispelling the peace she needed. She would be almost overwhelmed by the desire to tell her everything, about all the unfair anger and unreasonable embarrassment and the guilt.

Always she drew back. She didn't dare indulge herself in such weakness. It would be too painful for her wonderful, sensitive mother to learn that the daughter she was so proud of could ever have had such feelings. If she did confess it all, it might be the single unbearable thing that could bring it all back—that withdrawal, that silence, the end of joy and laughter. She couldn't take such a chance just to gain her mother's forgiveness and rid herself of her guilt.

Then, on the Thursday before the block supervisors' meeting, she got a failing grade on a math test.

The school year was drawing to a close, and her grades had always been good. She had even done well in math, her least favorite subject. At first when she saw the score of 59 percent on her paper, she knew it had to be a mistake, but when she checked the problems, it was clear that she had truly failed.

Mr. Arnold asked her to stay after class.

"Alisa, I cannot imagine what has gone wrong," he said. "I have been aware of your lack of attention for the past couple of weeks, but *this*—you can see for yourself that it was nothing in the world but carelessness that caused you to do so poorly. Whatever it is that's distracting you, can't you find a way to take care of it? This must not continue!"

Stunned, she only nodded and left the room. He was right about one thing: Something had to change. And of course she knew what it was, but she'd gotten nowhere alone. Resigned, dreading it, she approached Mrs. Birnam.

"I need some advice, some help," she said. "Could you . . . could I come in and talk to you sometime soon?"

"Of course you may," Mrs. Birnam replied, smiling. "How about this afternoon after dismissal?"

"You haven't discussed this with your father, either?" Mrs. Birnam asked when Alisa had haltingly described her distress. "From what you've said, he seems a very intelligent, understanding person."

"I couldn't," she replied. "He's had so much trouble already, and I was always afraid he would blame himself, because it all started after he lost his job. I couldn't stand that!"

Mrs. Birnam nodded thoughtfully. "Alisa, there are so many concerns with any illness like your mother has suffered that remain unspoken. Some of them are hard to face, such as a tendency to blame the person who's sick.''

"But I never did that!" Alisa protested. "How could it have been her fault? She didn't *want* to be sick! That isn't even logical.''

"I know, but I'm talking about things that might take place in our unconscious minds, and that isn't always logical in the conscious sense. For instance, you can see many physical disabilities. There's no tendency to assign any fault for a broken leg. But mightn't we possibly have an insidious feeling that someone who's depressed could pull himself out of it if he'd only *try* harder? Strange and illogical as it seems, it isn't at all unusual to feel that way, especially if the person who's ill is very close and the illness affects us deeply.

"And then there's the anger to deal with. It's clearly unfair to be angry with someone who's sick, or even someone we loved who has died. However, either tragedy is a kind of desertion. Alisa, the anger *happens*. It's normal. The problem is that we can't admit it and forgive ourselves, because on a conscious, practical level we know that it's unreasonable. So we try to ignore it, to cover it, to hide it from ourselves. And it makes us more miserable for not facing it.

"Furthermore, although I agree that blaming your neighbors and friends and teachers for their awkwardness concerning your mother's illness isn't very productive, there's no way in the world that you can avoid being affected by those things.

"Talk to your parents, Alisa. Tell them what

you've told me. Give them the opportunity to forgive you if that's the way you truly feel.''

''But I'm afraid. What if it's too much, what if it all sounds too cruel? Especially to Mom, but to Dad, too.''

''I don't know your parents well, Alisa,'' Mrs. Birnam replied softly, ''but I don't believe I've ever before heard anyone speak of her parents with such admiration and love. They won't be hurt, Alisa. They'll understand. And in your case, I suspect you won't be really at ease until you do talk it over with them.''

''I know. I've known it all the time, I guess,'' Alisa said, defeated. ''I wanted to find a way to avoid it. They've been through so much!''

''No more than you've been through. Don't you see, Alisa, that you've been trying to carry a burden that they should be sharing with you? They would be heartbroken to learn one day that you'd been so unhappy and didn't tell them, didn't give them a chance to help. Don't think of it as *taking* a chance; think of it as *giving* them a chance. They love you; it's their job . . . and it's what they want. I'm sure of it.''

She thought of little else for the rest of that day and the next. Then it was suddenly time for the meeting. Her parents were going to the meeting, too, but Paul came for her.

''My dad loved his judging assignment this afternoon, but he wouldn't tell me who won,'' Paul said. ''It's been great seeing him. And seeing Mom and Dad together, talking like good friends—I think I understand both of them a lot better now.''

"I'm glad, Paul," Alisa said. "It makes me so happy to know that you're sorting everything out and that you're not moody and angry anymore."

"How about you, Alisa?" he countered. "I know you've had something on your mind lately."

"You're right," she said, smiling, "but I think I'm about to get myself on track, too. Tonight I'm going to have a talk with my parents, and I'm sure that will help. I'll tell you about it afterward if you'd like to hear, but I really do think everything's going to work out all right."

He nodded. "Let's go somewhere tomorrow," he said. "A picnic! That's just the thing. No work, no worry. We'll just loaf and talk and eat and maybe even take a nap in the sun."

"It sounds wonderful. Marvelous," she said happily. "I'm already looking forward to it."

The church basement was already crowded when they arrived. People moved about, talking, looking at the wonderful before and after pictures, and having a good time. Paul introduced both his parents to Alisa, and then her parents arrived and chatted with Paul's folks. Mr. McLeary was there, and the mayor, and others whom Alisa didn't know. She recognized a photographer from the newspaper, and just before the meeting started, Mr. Reed came in, and Mrs. Birnam, too, with her husband.

"We wanted to be in on the conclusion," Mr. Reed said, giving her an unexpected hug and shaking Paul's hand. "You did it, kids! What a fine way to conclude the school year. Henry David Thoreau may be looking on from somewhere up there, too. He'd be as proud as I am of what you've done."

Then Ralph Carner stood up front and asked for quiet. "I think I speak for everyone here when I say that the past few weeks have been as fine as any in my life," he said, and the room erupted in cheers and applause.

"We could say an awful lot more tonight, but I guess we'd better get on with business," he said. "The block supervisors and others have asked me to thank everyone who helped us make our town look like a brand-new place. Thanks to the city, the radio station, the newspaper, Mister Art McLeary, Rutland Building Supplies, and all the residents, including the children!"

Again the applause and cheers drowned him out, until he held up a hand for silence.

"We've got two pieces of business tonight. First thing, we want Mister John Heyser to come up here and announce the competition winner."

Mr. Heyser made his way through the crowd and to the front. "The *winner* is the whole city of Rutland, every single citizen," he said, "and the new appearance of the town is the primary award. As to what you've asked me to do—judge the home improvement—well, I don't know when I've had a responsibility that I've enjoyed more. It wasn't easy to choose, but my choice is . . . Jack and Brenda Huggins of Six Thirteen Fifth Street!"

There were more cheers, congratulations, and applause. Alisa didn't see a single disappointed face. Evidently they were all too proud to be envious.

When the noise had settled once more, Ralph Carner stood up again. "Will you come up now,

Mister Reed?'' he called, and Mr. Reed, wearing a mile-wide smile, made his way forward to take Mr. Carner's place. He held something in his hand, but Alisa couldn't see what it was.

"I've been delegated to present another award tonight," he said, "and nothing could make me more proud. But first I want to explain that this award was authorized by all the block supervisors, and they all chipped in to pay for it. Now, listen while I read what's engraved on this plaque. I have two of them, and they're identical:

"The residents of South Rutland hereby express the deepest affection and appreciation to Alisa Wilson and Paul Heyser for service to their community that is beyond price!"

Alisa didn't feel too embarrassed at her tears, for she caught Paul wiping his eyes as they went up to accept the beautiful walnut plaques from Mr. Reed in an explosion of applause that seemed to shake the very walls of the church. They managed to say thank you, but that was all, before they were surrounded by people shaking their hands, hugging them, and thanking them. She caught a glimpse of her parents, smiling her way, and they too were teary-eyed.

Then finally it was over, and they were home.

"This award is probably always going to be the most important one I'll ever receive," Alisa told them when Marty and Darlene were in bed. "There's just one more thing that I need to be completely happy. I need to talk to both of you . . . to confess, actually. There are some things I need to tell you, to ask for your understanding.''

It wasn't easy; on the other hand, it wasn't as difficult as she had expected to tell them everything that had troubled her for so long.

"Oh, my darling!" her mother cried when she had finally said it all. "Those things you've felt . . . they weren't *wrong* at all. It's completely understandable, completely normal, and I should have realized that you might be having those kinds of problems and brought it up myself. But you never said anything, never gave the slightest sign. Oh, Alisa, I'm so sorry that you've been unhappy! But there's no reason to feel bad, I promise you. I love you so much. *We* love you!"

"And you're even more strong and courageous than we realized," her father said, "keeping all this to yourself, trying to protect us from hurt. Meredith, what have we done to deserve such a daughter as this!"

Their loving, understanding words and the safety and comfort of their warm embrace washed her pain away, and she smiled through tremulous tears. It was gone, all the hurt, the guilt, and the sorrow. She was well and whole at last.

Chapter Twenty-three

ALISA WILSON WANDERED into the backyard while she waited for Paul to arrive. The picnic basket was ready on the front porch, and he would be there soon.

She wasn't looking for anything, for she had all she needed, but then her glance fell on Marty's happiness plant. He had forgotten about it, apparently. Maybe that was because he didn't need it any longer.

She knelt, smiling to see how strong and full the plant had grown in three weeks. It had been wounded but not destroyed. It was wonderful, she thought, the way nature nourished living things, making them even stronger for resisting winds and storms and other stresses so they could grow to fulfill their destinies. The plant still had some room to grow, but it had achieved its mature shape.

Maybe there really was something behind the question Mr. Reed had asked all those weeks ago about a master plan. In some ways she was no closer to understanding it than she'd been then, but there was *something* in the individual human soul that would not be defeated. And maybe that was master plan enough.

About the Author

Nadine Roberts is a teacher of high school English in Naylor, Missouri. She has also written handbooks on taxidermy and stone masonry. Married with three children and six grandchildren, Ms. Roberts nevertheless finds time for boating and camping.